night hack

nightSHADE

4

carey decevito

This book is an original publication of Emberlust Press.

Decevito, Carey

Night Hunt / Carey Decevito / paperback edition

ISBN-13: 978-1-988806-18-1

Cover photography by Eric David Battershell

Cover design by Clarisse Tan, CT Cover Creations

Cover model: Chris Spearman

Edits provided by Karen Hrdlicka

Proofing provided by Joanne Thompson

For my daddy. We lost you too soon, but you were with me through this one just as I know you'll be with me for countless others. I love and miss you every day.
—your oldest baby girl

acknowledgments

First and foremost, where would I be without the unconditional support of my family and friends. *Night Hack* has been so long in the making. So much so, I thought I'd lost myself there for a hot minute. Where all of my books display a certain difficulty to get out there, this one was the most difficult. Losing someone to cancer is never easy, but losing one's self due to grief makes things increasingly harder. Thank you for understanding I needed the time to process, the ones where I've had to hole myself in some quiet corner to get things done, for cheering me on, and celebrating this most bittersweet win with me, when those final words were written.

Eric David Battershell—you're an indispensable cog in my book world. Thank you for being part of this journey since the beginning.

Karen Hrdlicka—you are the Chewie to my Han Solo. Your impeccable knowledge never ceases to amaze me, to make my wordsmithing shine.

Joanne Thompson—you've been there since practically the beginning. Thank you for your counsel, your insight, and calling me out on my shit when things aren't up to snuff. When you combine forces with Karen, you two are unstoppable.

Dearest bloggers, readers, reviewers & fellow authors—the book community is one that can sometimes be easy to get lost into. Thank you for your support, your continued readership, and most of all, providing me with the kick in the ass I've most definitely needed to finish this one. I try my best to support and share everything out there, and it definitely doesn't go unnoticed that you pay it forward. I'll forever be in your debt.

one

JANA

"9-1-1, my name is Jana, what is your emergency?"

"Yeah, this is Hank Berry...I'm at uh...217, unit B... Carolina Forest Boulevard...I need a cleanup service and...uhm...maybe a doctor."

What the fuck? I had an inkling, before beginning my shift, tonight would be one for the record books. And my instincts were right on the money. Overnights may kill my circadian rhythm, but they didn't lack for a bevy of interesting calls.

"Sir, are you injured?"

"Uh, I think so," the man groaned, "but I...I don't really know what's left."

My brows furrowed, but despite knowing I needed as much information from my caller as I could garner, I was hesitant to ask.

"What's left of what?"

"My wife was in the bathroom, so...uh, I figured I'd just go in the sink."

Sick, was my first thought. What grown man couldn't

fucking hold it in until his wife took care of business before tackling his own biological needs? Or better yet, try using the great outdoors like a hiker, or Bear Grylls? Still, I waited for him to continue and he sure as shit didn't disappoint.

"And I slipped on my own piss, and uh...caught my schlong in the sink drain."

"Sir?" I managed. I'm sure I'll be getting a good laugh out of the rest of the team on this one, but I was seriously feeling the contents of my earlier dinner creeping up for a good purge.

"I tried pulling myself up after falling onto the sink when the chair broke, but I hit the switch to the fucking disposal, and it turned on."

Oh, fuck me! Had I heard right? I managed to just barely cover up my wince, not to mention, I swallowed the lump of bile in my throat before uttering, "Wait...what?"

"Ma'am, I just...I just ground up my own cock, ma'am."

Putting my own discomfort to the side, because...*hello!* this dude just hamburgered his goods, and my normally impeccable filter crashed and burned as the following words spewed out of my mouth. "Are you serious?"

"Yes...ma'am. I just ground up my own dick," he repeated.

Unable to hide my shock and maintain composure, "Oh, my God!" was what came next.

"The disposal has disposed of my dick all over the walls!"

I swear, I couldn't make this shit up, even if I tried.

Triangulating the location of the call with the address he gave me to the nearest team of first responders—EMT and fire alike—I dispatched the call immediately, assuring the man on the other side of the line. "Hank, help is on the way."

"Ma'am, I have to warn you," he said sharply. "It's like the Tasmanian Devil went buck wild on some spaghetti in here."

I can't help but question where his wife is at this point in time as I haven't heard anything in the background as of yet, thus feeling rather stupid in saying the next. "Sir, if you'll unlock your front door, the EMTs will be there shortly to assist you."

"Aw, man...this is like the Slip n' Slide from hell," he groaned. To be honest, I was quite surprised he wasn't howling in pain. Then again, shock—which I supposed he had to have been suffering from—had a bizarre way of setting in for certain folks. "Fuck, I think I'm gonna pass out."

Next thing I know, a crashing noise and a loud thump followed.

"Sir? Sir?" I waited a few seconds. "Hank, can you hear me?"

Nothing.

Then the line went dead.

After that one call, I would have liked to say my night had gotten better. Along with the routine health and safety emergencies, throw in a couple of domestic disturbances, and some wellness checks, I had to deal with a slew of calls that were a complete misuse of what our lines were meant for.

By the time my twelve-hour shift ended, it was eight in the morning and my eyes could barely stay open. The next three days off would be well-spent, sleeping in and getting back on track for my next three-days' worth of dayshifts.

Before I could manage to leave my desk, my boss poked his head over my cubicle half-wall. "Janice." I winced at his use of my given name. "We need to talk in my office when you're done here."

"It's Jana, sir."

No acknowledgement. "Five minutes."

Unfortunately, when I started my job as a dispatcher for the Jacksonville's 9-1-1 service, and despite my being vocal about my preference for being called Jana, Steven Saxon had refused to call me by anything but my legal name.

"Be right there," I mumbled to vacant air, seeing as the man had already disappeared.

A few minutes later, I knocked on Steven's open door.

"Come in, Janice," he said while writing something on a stack of papers that appeared to be some sort of report. "Close the door."

"Sir?" I questioned as I did what he asked and took a seat in one of the chairs across from his desk.

"First." He put down his pen and closed the file he'd been engrossed in just moments earlier. "I know you're just coming off a night cycle but I just got a call from Dylan, and his wife had the baby."

"You need me on another night cycle?" As happy as I was for my coworker, I despised him just a tad in that moment. I could have used a cycle of days with how exhausted I was feeling. My boss nodded. "Okay."

"Thank you for being understanding, and I want you to know you being a team player hasn't gone unnoticed."

My brows moved up toward my hairline, my heart raced. *Could this be about—*

"Now, about that managerial position you applied for."

Yes! I've worked my ass off for the last six years to get here. I finally—

"We decided to bring in someone from the outside." My celebratory mood officially in the shitter, I felt myself slump low into the chair I occupied. "I know you're disappointed, and it wasn't an easy decision. You have a stellar track record here, and we view you as an asset with your initiative and dedication, but at this time, we think you'd be better on the floor, doing what you do best until such a time another managerial opportunity presents itself. I truly believe the others could stand to learn a thing or two from you. In the meantime, I've got Kyle starting on your next shift. I recognize it's not an optimal setup, as you were gunning for the same position he's now in, but I hope you'll be able to show him the ropes, per se."

Right. I only managed a whispered, "O-okay."

"Go home, mull things over, and if you have any questions for me, my door is always open."

On a curt nod, I got to my feet and mumbled a, "Sure, sir."

"See you in three days, Janice."

"Jana," I supplied over my shoulder.

"What's that?"

"Jana. I prefer Jana, sir."

"G'night, or good morning rather, Janice."

I sighed, then exited the man's office on a simple, "Later, boss."

Would things ever change in my favor?

BRYCEN

"Fuck off, asshat!" I cursed at the bevy of monitors before me.

My fingers pounded the keyboard while I attempted to stop the motherfucker's progress as he tried to crash the First Bank datacenter by sending him bits of code here and there.

I'd been hunting this bastard hacker for the latter part of the last six months, when Shane—a coworker and friend—had mentioned the guy had threatened to break into the FBI's databases.

For the life of me, I don't get why someone would even attempt to hack into the FBI or any other government agency's networks, for that matter, unless they were tasked to do such a thing for the sole purpose of pointing out vulnerabilities. Okay, sure, some do it for kicks, and don't get me started on those who spy for domestic and foreign agencies.

I won't claim to be the best, but I know my shit, and I don't always color inside the lines when it comes to getting my hands on those with nefarious intentions. I suppose you could dub me a red hat hacker, to my boss's wife—and cyber partner in crime —Devolin, or Huss, Hussy, and Dev for some of us. She's definitely more on the white hat side of things since meeting her husband, but her former talents sure helped me evolve into my current role.

When my systems stopped alarming, I knew the battle was over for now and I'd lost, albeit not entirely. Seconds later, as I dialed to alert the authorities, a text screen popped up on my main monitor—I have six of them going at the moment.

@STRA4EVA:

Better luck next time.

Next thing I knew, my systems crashed.

"Son of a bitch!" I cursed, getting to my feet, then unplugging everything. Damn good thing I wasn't hooked into NSI's mainframe. I never was when I chased the near-invisible. The last thing we needed was someone to rape our network, leaving us and our clients—some of them high-profile government contracts—vulnerable, for a lack of a better description.

"Hello?" I hear groaned on the other side of the line, almost forgetting I was sporting my wireless headset.

"This is Brycen Matthews from Nightshade Securities. My apologies for the late hour, sir, but it couldn't wait."

"Yes, Mr. Matthews. I expect you're not calling with good news at this time of night," the owner of First Bank responded.

"Unfortunately, not," I grumbled. "You've had a breach in your datacenter. I've managed to back everything up and shift it to that external one we've put together for you last month, but it's possible this guy has gotten his hands on some information, regardless of my efforts," I explained.

"Matthews, Mr. Kippers assured me you were the best to fortify our systems," the man hissed across the line. "What the fuck are we paying you for?"

"Sir, this isn't just a simple hacker we're dealing with," I sighed. If I didn't have to deal with people at all in this business, I'd be a much happier man. As it was, the man and his various boards were predominantly at fault here, having taken their damn time with giving the go-ahead on the data migration. "Rest assured, I'm on the job and I'll get to who's behind this."

"I hope so, Matthews, or it's yours and Kippers's asses on the line. I want answers yesterday, you hear me?" Without another peep and not waiting for a response from my end, the man hung up.

Next up, I needed to call my business partner and announce his livelihood might be at stake if I couldn't straighten this shit up and close that Astra dude down permanently.

"Yo!" Dalton's greeting came through, along with a baby crying in the background.

"Fucker got into First Bank. Mayer is in an uproar and my systems are down until I can get them fired up again," I blurted.

"The fuck are you still doing at the office, Matthews?"

I groaned, "Did you not—"

"I fucking heard you, Bryce, but I'm in the middle of things with a kid who just got shit all over himself and me while upchucking the bottle I just finished feeding him. He's got a fever, I have a wife who's down with the flu, and it's the middle of the night."

My brows scrunched up. "It is?" I looked to my watch to find that it was a little after two in the morning. "Fuck, boss. I'm sorry." That also explained the extreme temper I was met with from Mayer.

"Get that shit figured out. And by that shit, I mean your systems, then get your ass home," Dalton ordered. "I don't want to see your ass in the office until lunchtime."

"And Mayer?"

"I'll handle him first thing tomorrow. You know how clients get when shit hits the fan. We'll make it right and the man will cool his jets. It's his own fucking fault for not taking you and Dev up on your suggestions earlier anyway," he assured me, then mumbled a, "I don't understand how anyone gets anything done when they have to deal with the bureaucracy of a fucking board," before promptly hanging up.

I wasn't too sure about his ability to smooth things over with Mayer, but I'd trust Dalton Kippers with my life, so why not trust him to fix what I'd fucked up; then I'd make amends come tomorrow. After all, I had a quarter stake in NSI, so it wasn't just his livelihood on the line, it was mine and everyone else's.

two

JANA

"GOOD MORNING, SLEEPYHEAD." My brother Jason looked up from the thermos of coffee he was doctoring for himself.

"Afternoon," I corrected, considering the microwave clock reminded me I'd overslept as it was just past one twenty. "Sorry, I'm a little behind. How's Mom this morning?"

Sighing as he screwed the lid on his coffee, he proceeded with, "Same. Nausea's getting worse. Listen—"

"Not this again," I groaned, fetching myself a coffee mug from the cabinet. "It's not time, Jace."

"Don't you think we should at least put a plan together for when the time does come?"

"Not yet," I said, nudging him away from the single-cup coffee maker, setting my mug under the nozzle, popping the first K-cup I grabbed from the basket holding a bold variety, then pressing the button that would brew what I predicted to be my first cup out of a half dozen cups of java for today. "Steve's asked me to train this new manager…"

Jason's brows furrowed, and his posture straightened. "They passed you up again?"

As the Keurig sputtered its last few drops, I gave him a curt nod in answer, then proceeded to pour my favorite hazelnut-flavored creamer into the steaming hot liquid.

"Sis…"

"Don't say it." My gaze lasered onto him.

His hands came up in a peace-keeping gesture. "I was simply going to say that they're crazy for looking elsewhere."

I agree, big brother.

For once, I'd have loved to have spent my first day off lying in bed, sleeping, and gorging myself on cookies and ice cream. It's what I did when life served up a hefty dish of disappointment, or rather, what I used to do. But since Mom's breast cancer relapse, particularly in these last few months, I had no substantial time to wallow. Instead, I did what my mother would have told me to do—I picked myself up and kept fighting the good fight.

Because she can't.

My time would come. I knew it. I also knew if I couldn't put my foot down at work with certain people—my boss, mostly—I would forever be the *next in line* for a promotion. Yeah, I was a little soft in my professional pursuits. Funny how that didn't seem to apply to all other areas of my life, however.

Last night, I'd walked out of my office building, gave a half-assed wave to the security guard at the front desk, then drove home, all the while pondering why I hadn't argued with Steve about this latest turn of events. The first two times, I'd accepted his and management's decision on passing me up, but then again, the candidates had been far more experienced and quali-fied—*and* internal. Now, however, despite the numerous posi-tive reviews regarding my work, not to mention the additional training and experience I'd acquired, I had a hard time believing my boss's words.

"It's not like I ever expected a promotion to management to

be dropped into my lap, but I've given it my all, Jason." *And they'd given it to some outsider with who knows what kind of experience.*

"He's probably some telemarketer or service line rep or something. Bet you this is all he's been doing for the last decade of his life, and this is him trying to finally get into something with more excitement," he mumbled to Kiki, my Maine coon fur baby, giving her a good scratch under her chin. The cat simply looked up at me from the back of the couch as I reached into the freezer, a twinkle in her eyes before she dropped her chin back onto her front paws when Jason headed toward the front door. "In any case, sis, I say give it another six months. If that curmudgeon can't see your greatness from now until then, I say cut your losses and get out. Maybe it's time you put that nursing degree to good use again."

"Yeah." *But I don't want to because Mom needs me*, then I added, "Maybe."

Settling onto the couch, with my coffee and a miniature tub of Ben & Jerry's in hand—I know, I know...breakfast of champions, right—I met my brother's eyes.

"She'll probably sleep through most of the day." His eyes displayed the exhaustion that all of us were feeling these days. "Seriously, think on what I said."

"Yeah, yeah," I said as I shoved a spoonful of Chunky Monkey into my mouth.

"Sexy," he laughed. "That's some guy's wet dream right there, sis."

Nearly choking on my treat, I grabbed the nearest throw pillow and chucked it at a smirking Jason, mock-shouting, "Bite your tongue and get out of here, would you!"

Leaving the utensil in my mouth, I grabbed the remote and started to look for the latest episode of *Lucifer*.

I absolutely adored the satire, loved the plot, and Tom Ellis wasn't hard on the eyes, nor was Kevin Alejandro, or D.B.

Woodside for that matter. I had most likely an hour to myself before my daughterly duties beckoned.

By Tuesday afternoon, I was drained of energy and feeling defeated by the latest test results my mother's doctor had discussed with us. Let's not leave out I was also dreading my next shift at work. I'd be, for all intents and purposes, training my own manager, Kyle what's-his-name. It simply wasn't right. Nothing was.

But you agreed, without putting up a fuss. Who does that? Me, that's who, and I was going to suck it up. This one last time.

With a new go-getter outlook on my professional life, I made sure to dress comfortable, but in something that made me feel confident, which meant I was sporting some of my favorite lacy undergarments—a guilty pleasure of mine. I would need it tonight.

Half an hour before my shift was scheduled to start, I was at my desk, making sure my system and phone were logged on and in fully functional order. All was a go for when the clock struck eight.

Hitting the *Do Not Disturb* option on my phone, I got up and headed to Steve's office as per his request.

"Boss?" The man's head popped up, and I noticed he wasn't alone.

Some scrawny dude was sitting across from him, red hair, thick black-framed glasses perched on his nose, and I swear he blushed five shades of red in the few seconds he'd laid eyes on me. The kid barely looked freshly out of college.

"Oh, good!" Steve got up from his seat and motioned toward the slightly postpubescent, barely-an-adult male. "This is Kyle, our new manager. I want him to stick with you tonight and listen in on your calls to see how things roll here. Make sure to take him around and introduce him to the crew that's on schedule tonight. And Kyle," my boss turned his head to the man-child, "you're in phenomenal hands here. Janice has been with us for five—"

"Six," I interrupted the exchange. "Nearly seven, sir."

"Nearly seven years," the man parroted without looking my way.

So the man does listen! Therefore, I added, "And it's Jana."

Our superior sighed, then continued, "If you have any questions, Janice is the one to ask. Good luck, bud."

Bud? What in the ever-lovin' hell, who called a subordinate bud?

By the time midnight hit, it was clear the freaks were starting to come out to play. What else became quite evident to me was Kyle, who'd confessed Steve was his mother's first cousin, wasn't cut out for the job in the least, no matter how much managerial experience he may have had. To be honest, with the perplexed look on his face following each call I handled, I'd be shocked if the guy returned for his shift tomorrow night. If he couldn't hack it shadowing a dispatcher, he wouldn't survive as one—let alone cut it as their supervisor—which made him a piss-poor candidate to manage the group of us on any given shift.

I'd like to see how he would have handled Hamburger Dick the other night, I mused just as my phone rang.

Sighing, I focused on my screens, then clicked the pop-up for the incoming call. "9-1-1, this is Jana, what is your emergency?" I answered with my usual script.

I didn't hear an immediate response. Instead, I was met with heavy breathing, followed by gurgling.

"Sir? Ma'am?" I urged.

"K-kill-ing m-me," sounded in my ears, almost as though the person was trying with all their might to choke out their words.

"Ma'am, hold on for me. The EMTs are on their way." My fingers danced over my keyboard as I attempted to triangulate the call to get a location, hoping the connection lasted long enough for our systems to find where the caller was calling from. My system informed me the emergency was being rung via a mobile device.

It took approximately thirty seconds before I hit paydirt.

"Ma'am? You still there?"

"Dy-ing," she rasped, a wet sounding cough following her words, then a gurgle.

"What's your name, ma'am? Keep talking. Someone will be there to help soon." *Christ, please let her last another five minutes.*

More gurgling, but this time, I swear I heard the moment her last breath left her. Minutes later, still fused to the line, the sound of sirens could be heard in the distance. A moment longer, the line disconnected.

Help had arrived—I only hoped that it hadn't been too little, too late.

By the end of my shift, just as I'd guessed, Kyle was nowhere to be found. He'd excused himself at roughly around five in the morning, citing he needed to use the facilities. And the little rat bastard never bothered to come back. What was worse, my boss never bothered to check in with me either.

By eight, after having clocked out, I knocked on Steve's door.

"Gonna need you as acting manager until we find someone else," he grumbled by way of greeting. The man never had the audacity to even approach me to let me know my charge had left for the rest of his shift.

"Next in line, remember?" I told him, my inner feminist cheering me on.

The man's eyes widened, and his mouth opened and closed much like a fish out of water.

"Steve, you know I'm more qualified than anyone else on that floor," I argued, aiming my index in the general vicinity of the bullpen, where all the operators performed our duties. "Hell, I'll even start off as the nightshift manager and stick to it for the next year if it's what it takes."

"That's just insane." He crossed his arms over his soft chest, which only looked larger while sitting because his massive gut —due to too much fast food since his wife had left him— shifted upward. It wouldn't surprise me one bit if one of us would have to dispatch an EMT to our offices because the man looked one quarter pounder away from a heart attack these days.

I lifted my hand with my palm facing my superior. "Swear I will."

"That's unfair," he stated.

On a curt nod, I added, "You'd be right, but I'd do it just to prove to you I'm exactly what you're looking for. And don't get me started on the fact that Kyle was a family favor." I wasn't about to threaten the man about going to upper management for nepotism, but letting him know I knew about Kyle's family ties to him could potentially work in my favor, not to mention his own. "You said so yourself, no less than three days ago, I was the next best candidate. Save yourself the trouble of another job posting and several more interviews and let me handle things. Hell, you just asked me to act in the role! If you didn't trust my judgment and aptitude, then why would you ask, albeit, temporarily?"

His assessing gaze scanned me from head to toe. "All right." He nodded.

My lips tugged up into a wide grin. "Thank you, Steve. You won't regret it."

"I better not. This is your only shot, Jana."

"Hallelujah, he does know my name!" I joked. "Seriously, I'll have you wondering why you hadn't hired me in this role sooner."

The man's brows furrowed. "I'm not sure where this self-assured attitude came from since I saw you on your last night cycle, Janice Elway, but I'm hoping it sticks. You'll need that assertiveness to tackle the rest of the team."

BRYCEN

"Babyface, get your ass in here!" Dalton hollered, then slammed his office door closed.

Oh, fuck!

First, the man had to have been watching the monitors at his desk to know I'd just walked through NSI's main entrance. Second, he was miffed as all get out, judging by the slamming of his door. Third, no good conversation came from when he called me by that fucking nickname I despised so much.

Shuffling my feet to the man's office, I opened to find him bent over his garbage can, puking his guts up.

"My, have the mighty fallen?" I joked.

Bloodshot eyes pierced through me as Dalton grabbed a Kleenex and wiped at his mouth, throwing the soiled tissue into the puke-filled can. "Shut the fuck up and close the fucking door," he rasped.

"Why the hell are you in, D?" I moved inward after closing the door but stayed a good six feet away from the man. Whatever bug this thing was, it was a strong one if Dalton looked like he was knocking on death's door.

"Picking up a few things, mainly files, then heading home," he announced.

"Could have brought you that shit, bro," I told him.

"S'okay," he mumbled, leaning his head back on his chair, closing his eyes. After a few deep breaths, he opened his eyes and gazed over my way. "Good work on that First Bank account. Wanted to tell you Mayer called this morning and he's happy with the work you put into their systems to fortify them. Honestly, if I didn't know any better, I'd say you were channeling a little of my woman."

He wasn't too far off the mark. "Let's just say those little games we play," I referred to the times we hacked into each other's systems, "have definitely helped. Your woman might be on the straight and narrow now, but she's still got a clever streak a mile long. W-W-D-D."

"*W-W-D-D*? Fucker, stop that tech talk and speak English. I have a feeling I'm about to puke up my spleen next. Think I left my liver in that garbage bag when you walked in," he said.

"What would Dev do? W-W-D-D."

"Dork," he said as he picked up the garbage can once more.

"On that note..." I turned and headed toward the door as the man wretched again. "I'll go finish that report for Mayer. It should reassure him that his data wasn't stolen. Then, I'll be sure to have this entire office suite fumigated once you get out of here."

Dalton peered above the edge of the can at me. "Fuckin' right." On widening eyes, he jolted to his feet, an "Oh, shit!" wrenching from his mouth as he made a beeline for his office bathroom, still clutching the can in case he didn't make it in time.

I hurried the hell out of there before the plague got to me too. To make sure to eradicate any germs on my hands, I emptied about half the small hand sanitizer bottle from my desk drawer into my palm, not caring that it was dripping all over the floor.

Rather than go home after a day's work, I headed over to McAskill's, a bar owned and operated by an acquaintance of mine. This week, I'd been making a concerted effort to clock out at a decent time, if you can call seven a decent hour when I'd been hard at it since five this morning. But I had no interest in crashing on the couch, watching mindless television tonight, though.

I'm not what you'd call a social butterfly by any means, but I do enjoy people watching, and let's face it, I haven't eaten anything all day and one of Ben's burgers would do me just right in filling the growing pit in my stomach.

Finding a seat at the end of the bar, I'm properly positioned to see McAskill's patrons come and go. Apparently, I wasn't the only one with the same idea early on a Friday night.

As the raven-haired statuesque beauty that had some height to those voluptuous curves of hers let herself drop into the seat next to mine on a long sigh, I couldn't help myself.

"Long day?"

"More like a long week," she mumbled without looking my way.

"Hey, Matthews, got a new IPA on tap last week, you want?" Ben lifted an empty glass with his inquisition.

"Pour her generous, Ben, and get her anything she wants." I tilted my head in the woman's direction.

"Y-you didn't have to do that," she said, her cheeks filling with a subtle blush that intrigued me a little too much.

"No trouble. You look like you could use a couple."

Ben eyed her in question as he waited for her order. "I'll have what he's having and add your best bourbon chaser. One for him too, please."

"Brycen Matthews." She took my proffered hand and a frisson skittered from my fingertips, up my arm.

The woman's eyes widened, and her lips pursed. "Jana. Jana Elway."

Jana. A good name befitting an exotic natural beauty with a killer smile and curves to rival the world's best sports car. This night just got miles better.

JANA

My girls weren't able to come out and join me, but I wasn't going to let that stop me from celebrating my promotion. It's too bad the day had been shrouded with the news my mother's cancer had metastasized. To make matters even more difficult, the proverbial dark cloud had only grown darker when the crime beat in the local newspaper had been covering the very same call I'd handled with the choking, dying female on the daily since Wednesday.

One call.

Countless articles.

A single murder.

And I'd had the displeasure of being the operator for it.

You're here to celebrate, I reminded myself then proceeded to ask Ben, the owner it turned out, to get me and my lone wolf of a drinking partner, Brycen, a second round of his newest IPA and bourbon.

By one in the morning, I couldn't remember the last time I'd laughed so much in my entire life.

Brycen Matthews, although a pathological flirt who claimed he only spoke the truth, had turned out to be pretty easy on the eyes, with that dashing smile, surfer boy dirty-blond hair, broad shoulders, a killer sense of humor, and an intelligent wit to boot. His best feature though, was his eyes. Those brown orbs shone with truth and gentleness; they were smooth as chocolate.

"Give me your phone," Brycen requested as the night neared its end.

My brows met my hairline. "Why?"

"Because I'll program my number in it. You see, I don't get out much." His smile was self-deprecating as he whispered the next, "I'm kind of a workaholic. It's been a nice night, talking to a beautiful woman who was able to keep up with my shenanigans and put me in my place. I'd like to do it again sometime. That is, if you—"

A giggle escaped. With my latest promotion, I wasn't sure as to how much free time I'd have to myself, except for my off days, and even those were about to become an even bigger challenge. However, I knew, just from tonight, hanging out with Brycen wouldn't be a hardship in the least. If anything, he'd be good for my ego and a few laughs during some dark personal times. I wasn't looking for anything more than that because it just wasn't in the proverbial cards for me. I'd seen it with my folks, coworkers, and most recently, with my boss. No one can hold on to a decent relationship when their work demands such an unreliable change in schedules. Plus, after the disaster that was my last relationship? No, I didn't need it. But a good friend of the opposite gender? That, yes, *that* I could do.

When he handed me my phone back, his device pinged a few seconds later. Grabbing his phone, he hit a few buttons, then a few more with that teasing grin on his face. My cell began blasting "I'm Too Sexy" from my hand.

"You're quite pleased with yourself, aren't you?" I laughed while muting my device, then shoved it inside my purse without looking to see what he'd texted me.

He shrugged his shoulders. "It's my thing. The guys at work know it, and most of them get a kick out of it."

"You said you work in security, right?" Brycen had said as much but hadn't gone into any detail.

"I take care of the information technology side of things for Nightshade Security Incorporated," he explained what his role within NSI was. "There's Dalton and me as original owners, with Shane as a buy-in. Aside from us for staff, we have two full-timers, and the rest are all part-timers. We cover a wide range of services, really. We have retired military, an active police detective, a bounty hunter, who you'd listen to in a heartbeat because his ugly mug is a scary one, a search-and-rescue operative, and a few others with differing specialties."

"Wow!" I was truly impressed. "You own part of the company too? Good on you!" The look on his face spelled "ah shucks, ma'am" which was an endearing expression. The man at my side could dish out the compliments but didn't seem used to receiving them in return.

"It's nothing, really. I get to do what I love, and help the guys do their thing."

So modest too. "I'm sure you're selling yourself short there, Brycen."

His eyes dilated with heat. "I like you saying my name like that."

I shook the effect of his deeper baritone out of my head and smirked. "I should get going. It's been really nice chatting with you, and yes, we should definitely do this again sometime. Thank you for the drinks and the laughs." Before I could think otherwise, I leaned forward and brushed my lips against his scruffy cheek. "G'night, Brycen."

Walking out of the bar and toward one of the waiting cabs, I had enough time to jump in, giving the driver my address before my phone chimed with Right Said Fred's one-hit wonder.

I smiled as soon as the name popped up. *IT Dude?*

IT DUDE:

Good night, beautiful.

IT Dude? Seriously?

IT DUDE:

Fine, you can change it to handsome, sexy, or some other flattering nonsense.

I laughed out loud, the driver's eyes perusing me in his rearview for a short moment before the edges of his mouth quirked up in a smirk.

What about surfer boy?

IT DUDE:

Honey, I'm all man. There's nothing boyish in the least about me, I assure you. ALL. MAN.

Sporting a grin, I typed.

> Fine. 'Handsome man I met at the bar on
> Friday' it is.

IT DUDE:

Ha! I knew you thought I was handsome!

Before I could respond, another text popped up.

IT DUDE:

Okay, sweetheart, get home safe and text me
to let me know you got there. Preferably from
your bed. ;)

> You're incorrigible!

> And what if I did?

I bit my lip as I followed through with the next text. I was treading the deep end here, that proverbial line between friends and more, but I couldn't help myself.

> What if I did it nekkid?

IT DUDE:

You're killing me here.

I'm in the back of the smelliest cab, by the way.
I hope your ride is faring better.

FYI...I'll be answering in the buff myself. ;)

> It's the only way to sleep, isn't it? And nope.
> This cab stinks to high heaven with cheap
> cologne and week-old milk.

IT DUDE:

Mine smells of old farts and half-decomposed
salami.

Ew!

Well, I'm almost home.

IT DUDE:

Only halfway there for me.

Text when you get in.

I said I would. Jeeze! Demanding much?

JK!

IT DUDE:

Oh, you have no idea, sweetheart. ;)

Oh hell! My lady parts had been dancing on and off all night, despite the fact I had convinced myself that nothing but friendship would come out of this encounter with one Brycen Matthews.

A few minutes later, I paid the cab driver and let myself into my moderate-sized bungalow, Kiki greeting me at the door.

"Hello, girlie," I cooed, taking the time to scoop the feline up in my arms and buffing my cheek against her soft fur as I turned the deadbolt to the front door into the locked position.

A refilled bowl of water and a quick check on my sleeping mother later, I was in my bedroom, stripping out of my clothes before heading to my en suite bathroom. Teeth brushed, and settled on the cool sheets of my bed, I grabbed my phone, turned the camera's picture setting so it faced me, and brought the blankets up just so a single bare shoulder and my face were all you could see.

Safe, sound, snuggled. G'night!

It took a few seconds and I saw those bubbles that were the telltale sign of an incoming text.

IT DUDE:

Dead. :D

That's one lucky bed, by the way.

A cold one.

IT DUDE:

Now you're just being mean.

I couldn't help but laugh out loud. Kiki, who had joined me on the corner at the foot of the mattress lifted her head, giving me the stink eye as if I'd just woken her from an overdue nap.

Good night. Text when YOU get in.

IT DUDE:

Will do. Goodnight, gorgeous.

three

BRYCEN

CHRIST, this wasn't like me at all.

Sure, I'd been attracted to other women from the get-go, but never had I felt that instant connection with anyone before. And don't get me started on the incessant texting I've been doing over the last day or so. It's been so bad I rivaled the frequency of the average social teenager.

But I knew it would come to an end all too soon.

Tonight, as a matter of fact. That's when Jana's work cycle began. I knew she worked as a 9-1-1 operator. She'd been out celebrating a promotion to management the night we met. I also knew her new role would have her working overnight shifts for quite some time. It's one of those deals where she'd be on for three days, then off for three.

Aside from that, Jana never really shared much more about her life or her job, and I got it. To be honest, I doubted I could do what she did. Twelve hours of listening to folks call in for assistance on what usually was the worst day of their lives—that's heavy shit right there.

So, despite her warnings she'd be scarce for the next little while, and the fact she'd divulged she'd never felt lighter with all the laughing I'd been providing her since we'd met, I had a plan to make sure she had a bit of light in her day—or night—as the case may be.

"Earth to Baby—"

"Don't even finish that sentence." My eyes fixated on and pierced through Devolin, who was making her return to work after that nasty bout of flu her household had seemed to have succumbed to. Too bad Dalton hadn't seemed to fare better than he had last week when I last saw him.

She had the decency to look sheepish before she asked, "What's up with that goofy smirk on that mug of yours anyway?"

"Nothin'," I mumbled, slamming my phone onto my work-station, albeit, a little too hard due to the annoyance I felt. I reached for the latest client file, which had been left on my desk late yesterday afternoon. I knew all too well my pretending to be engrossed in the latest client's request for us to investigate their finances and catch who was funneling money out of the company's accounts wasn't going to deter the woman in the least. So I led with, "How's the baby?"

Devolin's brows scrunched up. "He's back at daycare today, which is good, because Dalton isn't doing so well. I had to take him to the ER last night because the big lug hasn't been able to keep anything down, much less water. Three bags of fluids later, four hours surrounded by that antiseptic smell, and I was glad to be on our way home."

Considering her health issues with lupus during most of her life, and the all-too-numerous times she'd been hospitalized before that because of leukemia, I can't blame the way she felt about her latest foray to the hospital.

Devolin's disgusted expression morphed into a smirk, solely aimed in my direction when I tried to resume my task. "Oh no! Don't you think you managed to skew me away from my initial question, mister. Who is she?"

"Who? What?"

"Seriously?" She crossed her arms over her chest. "Do I have to hack your phone to know what's going on, because you know I will." She would too. "Now out with it."

"Is nothing sacred to you, woman?"

"If you count the mind-blowing orgasms your boss gives me on the daily, sometimes—"

I threw the file in my hands down onto my desk and plugged my ears in that universal childish reaction people do when they really didn't want to hear what's coming. "La-la-la-la! Shut up, Huss! I don't need details about D's junk and how he uses it."

"You're such a child."

My hands fell from my ears as I grinned. "And you're not?"

"Why won't you tell me?"

"Because if I do, the whole band of merry men who work here, and their women, will descend on this place for the Grand Inquisition," I told her. "I don't know what it is, or if it's anything at all, so I'm keeping it to myself until I'm good and fucking ready to spill the beans, all right? Besides, why would anyone like her want a workaholic like me? I'm married to my job right now, and I'm okay with that." *Sort of.*

Devolin's eyes widened while her lips formed an unmistakably surprised O. Winking at me, she turned toward her workstation and proceeded to drop her purse in one of the file cabinet drawers to her desk, firing up her systems. "Gotcha. But on a serious note," she said, concern and honesty in her gaze, "if you ever want to talk—"

"Yeah, yeah. You're here, Ember's here. The whole gang is here for me, right?"

Her, "Right," came at the same time Rex walked into our technology hut, barking, "When did you lose your man card?"

"Shut up. What do you want? I thought you weren't in until Thursday?" I asked him.

"Had to pick up something before I take off to hunt down a skip."

"Be safe out there," Devolin said.

"Ain't no fun in that, Huss," he returned.

"Let us know if you need anything," I told him. The man gave me a curt nod and then turned to leave. "Later."

"Later." From down the hall, he added, "Find out who she is, Dev. Got a hundred for you if you get the deets before I'm back with that crazy bitch who tried to run over her husband last week."

I turned to give Devolin the evil eye, only to find her shoulders bouncing with mirth, her back facing me.

I'm fucking screwed.

JANA

"Jana, I could use you here," I heard as I walked toward my desk after a quick break on Tuesday night.

Those words had me freezing mid-step, the high from my quick text exchange with Brycen vanishing in that moment.

I approached Diane, one of the overnight operators. "You sure?"

She nods. "She's asking for you specifically."

"For me?" Snapping my fingers, I pointed to her extra headset. "Please."

As soon as the headset was on, I nodded to Diane so I could take over as she pressed the button to unmute my headset. "9-1-1, this is Jana, how may I help?"

My skin crawled. My heart rate accelerated, and I grew dizzy as I heard the telltale sounds of someone, most likely choking on their own blood. God, this was just like last week. Raspy, fluid-filled wheezes intermingled with that similar productive, wet coughing came through.

"P-please h-help me."

"Miss? Can you tell me where you're hurt?" I took note that Diane was still working to triangulate the call.

"H-hel—"

Just as Diane dispatched the first responders, I heard what sounded like a blunt thud, not quite like hitting, but similar, then the woman heaved, and the line went dead.

By eight the following morning, I could barely think straight. I was dealing with my normal level of exhaustion but add to that a visit from a Detective Peters, one of Jacksonville PD's finest, and despite how tired I felt, I was afraid I'd never sleep again.

The good detective had come to take my statement. Much like I had last week at Steve's instruction, I'd located the call's recording on our servers and provided Detective Peters with a copy. It was now up to him and his FBI counterpart to make the decision on if these two cases were related. In my personal opinion, and because I'd witnessed both calls audibly, I'd say the MO—or modus operandi—looked far too eerily similar.

What I wanted to know was, if these cases were linked somehow, why was I at the center of it all? And how had this latest victim known my name? Detective Shane Peters didn't have any plausible hypotheses for me but assured me that he'd be getting on it and would keep me updated.

Leaving me with his business card, he'd instructed me to give him a ring if any more calls of a similar nature—meaning ones with personal requests for me as their operator—came through or if anything that seemed or felt *hinky* happened.

Unfortunately, later that day, after I'd just started my next shift, is when *that* something came my way.

BRYCEN

"Incoming!" Dalton announced as he walked into the tech hub Devolin and I seldom left, unless we were called into a meeting or on our way home at the end of our workday. It was Thursday, and the boss was showing no sign that he felt like he was knocking on death's door less than a week ago. "I need you both in the conference room. Give me ten to rally up the rest of the troops."

Devolin turned to face me once her husband disappeared around the corner, and I recognized the look on her face. It was probably the same one that was currently strewn across my own mug. It's the one that boasted excitement because meetings like this were infrequent and normally meant a case had surfaced which would require a significant amount of our expertise.

"I should have known something was up when Kip told me Shane was coming in at lunch," she said.

"Oh, fuck. How much you want to bet we're being brought into those bank robbery cases that've been in the papers for the last month?" I rubbed my hands together. "Or maybe it's that—"

"Matthews, Shane doesn't do white collar crime." Devolin's face was pale, her eyes as big as saucers at her own realization.

She was right.

The man worked homicide.

Then the image of the story on the front page of the *Jacksonville Times* yesterday morning floated to the forefront of my mind. Murdered women. Two to be exact. Same MO, same everything as far as the media had reported.

"Let's go." Devolin hopped to her feet, stretched her back out, then headed out of our nook. I followed suit a minute later.

A possible serial murder case.

A homicide detective and his FBI liaison.

A 9-1-1 operator in potential danger.

What a fucking clusterfuck.

All of this had me thinking of Jana. I wondered if she knew who this Janice Elway woman at the heart of this sick fuck's obsession might be. I'd make a point to ask her next time I texted her—or better yet, when I saw her next—because this whole case had me feeling antsy.

While I was put in charge of monitoring the dispatch phone systems, Devolin was running a trace on the 9-1-1 call recordings. Unfortunately, they were the victims' which meant that Dev's job would be next to impossible. Both calls had originated from isolated locations around the city, and each had come from a different device, with no discernible pattern for location. The dispatch center's triangulating software was good, but only gave a general direction. The victims had never mentioned their exact location, and by the time EMTs had gotten to them, they'd already expired.

"This guy's totally sick," Devolin announced.

"Any headway on anything?" I asked.

"Not much right now. I don't know who this chick is, but it wouldn't surprise me if she decided to move to some remote location or holed up somewhere. I wouldn't wish being on the receiving end of any of these calls."

I agreed and added what I'd discovered, "What's interesting is that she's not like any typical woman. Her personal information is unlisted. She's got no social media accounts. No listed phone numbers, emails, or address. Nothing."

"Shit, she's good at keeping a low profile, so that's not how this monster's gotten her name. Did you look at DMV records, other government organizations? Hell, what about banking?" Devolin suggested.

Looking at the clock, I knew if I started that part of my research now, there'd be no way I'd be out of here before nine tonight, so I adopted the "it's a tomorrow problem" adage. "First thing tomorrow," I said, as I proceeded to dump all the information I had managed to get into the virtual file folder everyone working this case would be sharing. Noticing Devolin still looked pale, I added, "You okay with working on this?"

Next thing I knew, something slammed into the back of my head before finding itself thudding onto the carpeted floor. "Son of a bitch!" Looking down, I rubbed at the back of my head, finding a half-eaten apple.

"Serves you right for thinking I'm some delicate flower who can't handle this shit, Baby—"

"All right! I get it. Still, I just figured I'd ask," I said, then smirked, nodding to the discarded food. "Now pick up your trash, you litterbug."

"You deserved it."

"Fine. I deserved it, okay. Forgive me?"

"Only if you tell me who the hot number is that you've been talking with over the last week."

"No dice." I got up, headed toward the door to our hub. "Want a coffee before I take off for the day?"

"Get me a Barq's from the fridge instead. With a glass of ice."

"It's barely six and you're going on your third can of that shit. You sure you're not knocked up again?" I managed, then made myself scarce by rushing for the hallway before she chucked one of her keyboards at me next.

"Fucker better not have," I heard her mumble as I walked away, only to stop dead in my tracks once I turned the corner to the reception area.

four

JANA

"JANA?" I heard Brycen's voice, but with the way things had been since last night and this morning, just the slightest sound practically had me jumping out of my skin, Brycen Matthew's voice not exempted.

"Hey," I managed with a soft voice. It's a miracle I was able to talk at all what with my current state of exhaustion. In all honesty, I hadn't gone to bed yet. "T-this is where you work?"

"What are you doing here?" he asked, coming to a stop directly in front of me. "Are you okay?" I couldn't bring my eyes to meet his, and he must have known this as he reached toward me, a gentle hand tilting my chin up so our gazes connected. "You don't look so good."

"I came to drop this off." I lifted the small envelope from my purse and pressed it into his chest. "I, uhm...Detective Peters told me to come here and hand it over because it's evidence."

His brows furrowed as he looked down at the miniature yellow manila envelope I'd handed him, then back to study my face. "Evidence?" His fingers palpated the yellow manila envelope as if attempting to figure out what was inside it.

"For the 9-1-1 murder case," I croaked. "A third call came in last night, asking for me specifically."

"The fuck!" he roared, making me jump back. I wrapped my arms around myself, not that it would protect me from the demons haunting me after what I'd witnessed. "Oh, shit!" He folded the envelope and pocketed the thumb drive I'd saved the call on in the back of his jeans, then gently grabbed my shoulders, ushering me backward. He guided me to take a seat on the reception sofa. "I'm sorry, Jana. I-I didn't mean—"

"S'okay," I slurred, keeping my head down.

"No, it's not." His hand cupped my cheek, and I managed to look up at him. "Fuck, sweetheart, why didn't you tell me? You know what I do for a living, I could have—"

I shrugged my shoulders, then licked my lips. "The cops had it handled, or so I thought. Detective Peters told me to come here because he had a meeting with a Dalton Kippers?"

"So, you're Janice Elway?" he asked.

"Mmm." I nodded. "I prefer Jana."

"Okay." He paused, then reached for my hands, which was when I realized I was picking at my fingernails again—a nervous habit of mine. Pulling them apart, Brycen lifted them to his lips, kissing each of them before keeping hold of them in his. "Here's what we're going to do."

"But I was told to speak to a Devolin," I argued.

"Wrong. You're going to talk to me. You're going to tell me everything, then I'm going to cross-reference your story with the case files Shane dropped off earlier today. I want to know where you've been since we last saw each other, who you've visited with, the hours you've worked, which now I've got since I know it's you, and what your normal routine is like. Everything, Jana."

I'm sure my eyes looked as if they were about to bulge out of my head. "Brycen, I don't think you're that hot surfer guy anymore," I blurted.

That charming flirtatious grin of his came out, and it took

everything in my power not to collapse into the man's chest. This is as close to safe as I've felt over the last week.

"I-I think someone's been following me."

"Then you're going to come with me. Right now. We're going to head into the conference room, and then I'll rally some of the team members so you can speak to all of us directly," he explained.

"What about Devolin?" I wondered aloud.

"Devolin is right here," a female voice interjected. "I was wondering where you'd gotten to, Baby—"

"Huss!" he warned, then rolled his eyes, blushing as his gaze returned to mine. "Devolin, I'd like for you to meet the 9-1-1 operator at the heart of our newest case. This is Janice Elway. Jana, this is Devolin Kippers."

"Nice to meet you," I said as Brycen still held my hands in his and didn't seem to want to let go, even for this introduction.

Devolin's eyes aimed themselves first to my gaze, then to our joined hands, and then a grin spread over her face. "Wish it was under better circumstances, but you'll definitely do." With no fanfare whatsoever, she pivoted on her heel and walked away. "I'm getting the guys. Conference room in five, Babyface!"

I'll do? I wondered but, "Babyface?" was what came out.

And just when I thought I couldn't get any dizzier...

BRYCEN

"Babyface?" Jana asked.

I shook my head, took a deep breath, and cursed Devolin and her loose lips. "It's a nickname the guys here gave me years ago," I grumbled.

A cute giggle escaped her, making my eyes shoot up to meet hers. Jana's coloring had come back a bit with a slight pink tinge to her cheeks.

"I like that." I smiled.

Her brows furrowed. "What?"

"Your laugh," I explained. "Looks like you needed it too. Now, come on. Let's get this meeting done and over with so I can take you home."

"Huh?"

"It's either me or Rex. We're the only two available for surveillance work tonight, and now that I know it's you, there's no fucking way I'm letting him take care of my woman," I snarled, righting myself to my feet, then pulled Jana along.

"Your woman?"

As soon as her words were out, I realized what I had said. Coming to a complete halt, I spun around so fast that Jana crashed into my front. Steadying her with my hands on her waist, all I could do was stare into her wide eyes.

I expected embarrassment, regret...something akin to panic —much like what I witnessed in Jana's eyes right then—but I was met with a sense of calm and a deep feeling of rightness, so I gave her a curt nod and said, "Yeah, my woman." I grabbed her hand, then pulled her the rest of the way into the conference room. She'd just have to let the idea grow on her because I wasn't going anywhere until this case was solved, and even then, I doubted that would be sufficient enough time for me to have figured out why I couldn't get her off my mind.

"Dev just gave us the news," Dalton announced. "Matthews, you'll be on protection duty for the next few days."

"What about my mother?" Jana asked.

The men around us looked confused, and I'm pretty sure I shared the same expression.

"We live together," she explained. "She's too sick to live alone and—"

"Who's looking after her now?"

"My brother, Jason and I take turns," she said. "We trade off on our shifts."

"Jesus, woman, do you ever sleep?" Rex blurted.

As I squeezed Jana's hand in mine, she shot a self-deprecating smirk in Rex's direction. "When my mom does," she stated.

"Fucking saint," he mumbled as Dalton added, "Your mother, brother, and yourself will be fine staying together, Miss Elway."

"Okay," she whispered. "Now, how do I explain this to my family? Jason doesn't know all of what's been going on at work. I've barely had the time to catch up on how Mom's doing before he has to run out the door for work. How am I supposed to break the news that there's a-a fucking psycho that's calling me at work, making me listen in on his killings?"

"We've got it covered," Rex said, and I gave Jana's hand another reassuring squeeze, which she returned. Dalton seemed to have noticed the act as his eyes turned to me with a glint of recognition in them. "Bryce and I will go with you. We'll sit down, first with your brother, then we'll work on breaking the news to your mother without causing too much stress."

"She doesn't do well with change. What if we need to be moved?" Jana asked as opposed to argued.

"I'm a trained paramedic," Cade announced. "If it makes you feel better, I can be there whenever is most convenient for you, your brother, and your mother. Let's not borrow trouble for the time being, however."

"It's not that. I'm a trained nurse, but—" Jana shook her head as she cut herself off, then nodded in agreement. "Fine. And what about my job?"

"Since you're at the center of all this, it would be wise that you keep working. You're our main contact to be able to trace this guy," Rex explained.

"But if it all becomes too much," I interjected, "and you

need some time off, we'll do everything we can to keep you safe and help out the JPD and FBI with this case."

Dalton gave her a reassuring smile. "We'll get to the bottom of this, Miss Elway."

"Jana, please," she stated.

He nodded. "Jana."

"So what are you gonna do with Bailey?" Cade asked me, the men's curious gaze aimed at me, along with Jana's confused one.

"Who's Bailey?" Jana asked.

Turning to her for my explanation, I said, "He's my one-year-old, Aussie-German shepherd mix."

Her eyebrows knitted as she processed this. "But why would there be an issue with looking after—"

"You'll have someone with you around the clock," Dalton stressed.

"Sweetheart." I waited until Jana looked at me. "They're curious because I'll be with you, and the poor mutt gets into trouble when left to his own devices for too long."

"But—"

"Better safe than sorry," I explained.

"If it makes you feel any better, we can post him outside your home until things are back to normal," Rex smirked at his suggestion, which lacked appeal.

"Hey, that's not half bad," Cade chimed in, then turned to me. "That way you'd be able to take Bailey with you."

"And if you need anything, Jana, Bryce will be just a quick call or text away," Dalton added on a nod of approval.

I couldn't help myself. I reached up and cupped her cheek in my hand, her eyes tearing up.

"O-okay." Grabbing the hand that cradled the side of her face, Jana's eyes searched mine right before she threw herself at me, wrapping her arms around my neck in a hug. "Thank you."

The fruity scent of her hair had me closing my eyes, reveling in the contact between our bodies. Something about this arrangement niggled at me because I would have preferred to have watched over her from inside her home. Despite this, I rumbled a soft, "You're welcome, sweetheart."

Dalton and the rest of the men in the room seemed to be humored that I wasn't going to be making inroads with the woman in my arms by protecting her inside her turf. Not tonight, anyway.

Just please don't let me fail.

five

"WHAT IN THE hell do you mean there's a fucking psychopath after my sister?" Jason yelled.

"Mr. Elway—"

"Jace!" I scolded my brother at the same time Dalton spoke.

My big brother turned on his heel, his fury solely directed at me. "How long has this been going on? What did you do?"

"I didn't do—"

"Nothing," Brycen interrupted, then made to approach me, but I shook my head. Now wasn't the time for my brother to discover I had a budding *anything* with one of NSI's team members.

"Until we can get a grip on who this perp is, we need you and your family secured," Dalton stated. "I assure you, it's for the best."

"For the moment, we are tracking all methods this guy has used to contact your sister, but since her digital footprint is next to nothing, it'll take some time to locate him," Brycen added. "Trust me, I'm doing everything I can to keep her...*you all* safe."

Jason turned to Brycen, his arms crossed over his puffed-out chest, looking as though he was the greatest defender of all time. "And you expect me to have faith in some surfer—"

"No, *we* expect you to have faith in your local and federal judicial system," Dalton interjected, clearly at the end of his rope. "This isn't our first contract with JPD, nor do I expect it to be our last. You don't have to like it, but it is what it is. JPD is stretched thin enough as it is, and the FBI is in this in a strictly advisory capacity unless this case blows up and is officially declared a serial. That's where we come in."

"I need you to be on board with this, Jace," I said, sounding far too defeated than I'd have liked. "I know it's not ideal. And with Mom in the shape she's in—"

"And that's the part that has me worried, Jan. I know this isn't your fault, but did you stop to think about what this could do to Mom's health?" He began pacing in front of us, and all I could do was watch him diffuse his frustration and obvious worry onto the carpet. "Her immune system is going to take a hit with this coming and going of random—"

"Jace, I know you're worried about Mom. So am I," I began. "If I thought there was an easier alternative, I'd have argued with Dalton and his team. As it is, you won't even notice anything is amiss. Brycen will be outside, watching the house, and when he's gone, Rex who you'll meet tomorrow, will be here."

"And if neither of those two can make it, then one of our other men will be on task," Dalton assured. "Our part in this isn't to disrupt your everyday life. You'll keep going about your daily lives as you have been."

Jason turned abruptly to face the head of NSI. "And you'll stay on top of Jan at all times?" After a few seconds, my brother turned my way and studied me. With a resolved expression, he gave me a curt nod. "So, what's the plan?"

· · ·

"I'm so glad you have these friends, dear," Mom patted my cheek as Cade and my brother settled her down on the sofa.

"Are you comfortable, Mrs. Elway?" Cade asked.

"Oh, pish, I'm fine, young man," she stated, then wagged her eyebrows at me. "Where'd you find all of these fine young men, baby girl?"

My face burned as Cade tried to stifle his laugh unsuccessfully, probably more due to Jason's look of mortification. Even Dalton's—the ever-serious man I'd discovered he was—lip quirked up on one side.

"Seriously, Mom?" Jason whined.

"Oh, Son, I'm not dead yet, and even a blind lady could figure out how handsome all these men are just by their sheer baritones." She sighed for dramatic effect.

"All right, I give," Cade started. "Jana, I think you can handle this little spitfire yourself, but let me know if you need anything. I'll leave my work schedule on the kitchen counter for you. You'll find that I've set mine up so I can sub in when you're at work. That way, your brother will have some extra hands if needed."

All I could do was nod at his impeccable timing, but then wondered how in the world he knew what my shifts were going to be.

My confusion must have shown on my face because Brycen explained, "I called your boss and asked for a set schedule."

I stared at him, my brows rising. "Oh."

"I'll be back later to drive you to work. Meanwhile, I'll be out there," he said before dropping a quick kiss to my temple, then turned, heading out on Cade's heels.

"Before I leave," Dalton interrupted my whirling brain, "I have a few housekeeping rules for all three of you." He was the only one left. "First, tomorrow, or the day after, this house will be outfitted with one of our best security systems. Individual codes will be provided for each of you. Memorize them, then destroy the piece of paper they were written on. From that moment forward, you'll be using them as much when you're home as when you are away. Second, once the system is installed, you'll notice that your TV's channel three will be set to the security system. I don't want anyone answering any door without checking things out first."

In another situation, in another universe, I'd be laughing at the automatic nods my brother and mother provided the man. It's as if Dalton Kippers was a master puppeteer, manning the strings attached to their heads.

"Third, whenever either of you are heading out with Jana, you'll have your own escort. As I said, Jana living with you both is conditional, so long as things don't escalate. To safeguard everyone in this house, one of my men will be going wherever she goes. And lastly, if anything seems off, trust your gut. I'd rather get a call in the dead of the night that pulls me from my wife and kid for some stupid noise than get a call during daylight hours saying something serious has happened."

"Are you sure this is all necessary?" Mom asked, her eyes having rounded as wide as saucers.

"Ma'am." He paused, then smiled. "I assure you, if you were my family, I'd most likely still feel as though this isn't enough."

"O-okay," she stammered, her gaze widening as it met mine.

"I'll leave you to your evening, then," Dalton said as he took his leave. Pausing at the living room's entrance he added, "Jason?"

"Yeah?"

"A word outside, please."

My brows furrowed as my gaze met my brother's, but he simply shrugged, then followed the man out.

What the hell is that about?

Brycen was most likely minutes away from providing me with an escort to work. No sooner had the thought occurred, the doorbell chimed. Next thing I knew, a key in the deadbolt turned, and Brycen had let himself in.

This is going to take some adjusting, I thought as I simply stood there, gawking at the man and his show-stopping grin. Before any of us said anything, Jason joined us to see who had rung.

"There's been a change of plans. Our man, Rex, should be here in a few hours to introduce himself," Brycen announced.

Jason nodded, rumbling a, "Sounds good," then turned for the kitchen without another word.

"Forgive him," I said. "He's still grumpy that he can't be my savior. You know, typical big brother gig." I tried to smile, but judging by Brycen's sympathetic look, I'd say it came off looking forced.

"I can only imagine. If the same thing happened to one of my sisters, you can bet your ass I'd be grouchy too," he confessed. "Ready?"

I nodded. *As ready as I'll ever be.*

BRYCEN

There was no way in hell I'd get through this in the next few hours—even with Devolin's help. As it was, Mr. and Mrs. Kippers were off for the evening, and I was the one on-call. Then again, when one of our largest clients called you about funds being misappropriated, I knew the job would inevitably fall on my shoulders.

That also meant I needed to put someone else in charge of Jana for the end of her shift.

"Yo," Rex answered after two rings.

"Listen, I need you to handle getting Jana home after work," I explained. "Case just dropped and since Dev is off, I need to get the files up and going for an audit."

"Got it. Seven thirty?"

"She gets off at eight, so yeah. I'll let her know you'll be the one to pick her up. Thanks, man."

"Hey, it's no skin off my nose, bud. With a looker like that, it's one of the few perks of the job." He hung up, letting me stew in my frustration and, dare I say, a shit ton of jealousy.

Within seconds, my phone pinged in my hand with a text:

REX:

Relax, asshole. I know she's yours. :p

Respect, jackass.

I knew I didn't have to say anything. As much as my coworker behaved like a Neanderthal, he'd been nothing less than respectful of any and all of our clients, and especially the guys' women, throughout the years. Like Cade's girlfriend, Aspen, would say—a veritable teddy bear.

$$six$$

THE LINES WERE busy as they often were for a Friday night. Last night had marked my first week with my security detail. It felt strange, and even stranger still when I learned Rex had been put in charge of fetching me from my shift.

Once more, Rex had been the one to show up to chauffeur me to my job again tonight.

I hadn't heard much from Brycen, aside from the short texts letting me know he was busy with another client who required his expertise. Other than that, the playful exchanges we'd been sharing prior to my being entangled with NSI had abruptly halted.

Truth be told, I missed those messages. They'd been a semblance of normalcy and short-lived joy for me during otherwise monotonous and sometimes dreary moments—a little bit of light to each day.

Grabbing my phone, about to head on my break, I planned to initiate contact for once instead of letting him be the one to touch base.

"Hey, Janice," Steve called me as I walked by his office, "this package was delivered for you earlier today. If you're heading for your break, I'll just leave it at your desk."

"It's Jana, Steve, and thanks."

"Right. Sorry, Jana. Old habits and all that." He got up and grabbed the parcel that was on the table just inside his office's entrance. "I'll leave it on your chair."

With a singular nod, I hightailed it to the break room with my nose stuck in my phone.

> It's nearly midnight and I'm taking my first break. Just thought I'd check in, but I'm secretly hoping you're in bed and not locked away in your techno dungeon.

Within seconds, those telltale bubbles began to play about on my screen, indicating he was writing back.

IT DUDE:

Hey, gorgeous. In bed but far from asleep.
How's your shift?

> Busy with regular beginning-of-weekend shenanigans, enough to be entertaining for once.

IT DUDE:

Does that mean nothing hinky?

> Thankfully, no, but I did get a parcel in today's mail.

Bubbles, then they stopped. Then the bubbles resumed.

> Not sure what it is, because I haven't opened it. It's odd, I never have anything delivered here.

IT DUDE:

Do me a favor?

> What's it gonna cost? ;)

IT DUDE:

I'm trying to be serious here. Now you've got my brain going a mile a minute, trying to avoid putting my foot in my mouth with something entirely inappropriate, seeing as I'm supposed to be on your protection detail.

Part of me felt disappointed with his statement. Since when had we become so platonic?

Probably since you ran to him with your troubles? I had, but then again, I hadn't. I'd only done what the good detective had asked of me. The rest had been taken out of my hands.

I'd rather you stuck that foot in, if you please. :D

IT DUDE:

The professional in me would tell you not to open it until Rex or I are there with you.

More bubbles.
And the other side of you?

The other would ask if you'd perhaps ordered something to treat yourself on those cold lonely nights and mistakenly had it sent to the office instead of your home? The weather is getting chillier these days.

I laughed.

Oh, honey, we both know I sleep in the buff, remember? That applies to even the coldest of nights.

Okay, so I liked toying with him this way. Despite not wanting a relationship, a woman could still indulge her sense of attraction to the opposite sex every now and again. And Brycen Matthews was safe.

IT DUDE:

Gorgeous, as much as I'm enjoying your
playfulness, I need one thing from you
right now.

Oh?

IT DUDE:

Please wait to open that parcel. I'll be there to
pick you up at the end of your shift.

And what if I don't?

IT DUDE:

Fu$% that! Just humor me, 'k?

Mmm...maybe? Text later. Gotta head back to
work.

After a quick bathroom break, followed by making myself
another cup of coffee, I walked back to my desk, smiling as I
knew my lack of assuaging his concerns was inciting Brycen to
continue with a myriad of additional messages.

IT DUDE:

Don't. Open. It.

I swear, if you open that thing before I'm there,
I'll...well, I don't know what I'll do yet, but my
hand is itching here.

A spanking. Yes, that's what you need. :D

You make me crazy, woman.

In all seriousness, Jana. I'm worried. Please
wait.

Disregarding every subsequent message popping up, I
grabbed the pair of scissors from my desk drawer and slit the
tape at the top of the box, removing some of the brown packing

paper that covered whatever item it was. As the contents came into view, I froze, dropping everything like a hot potato. A blood-curdling scream that I never could have imagined coming from me rang through the open-concept floor.

BRYCEN

Goddamnit! That bloody woman was driving me insane, and I doubt she was trying to do so on purpose. As much as I was attracted to her, I had decided, for the foreseeable future, I'd try to maintain a slightly more professional stance. Of course, her fucking teasing texts made that incredibly hard, so I played her little game because hell, as much as I shouldn't, I couldn't help myself. We'd established that part of our relationship—or whatever you could call it—before her world had turned to hell.

When Jana messaged less than fifteen minutes after she'd gone offline, I knew she hadn't heeded my earlier warnings.

JANA:

Need you ASAP.

Stay where you are. I'm on my way.

Without wasting any time, I jumped out of bed, into a pair of jeans, grabbed my Sig P365 from the safe in my closet, tucked it in the back waistband of my pants, then grabbed the first T-shirt in my dresser drawer. Remembering I needed socks and shoes, I hurried further, grabbed my keys, locked up, then high-tailed it as quick as my foot and gas pedal could get me to Jana's office building. What should have taken me half an hour, even at this late hour, took me twenty.

"Where is she?" I growled to her boss as he escorted me beyond the security desk in the building's main lobby.

"I put her in the quiet room we have reserved for those that need to get away after nasty calls. Follow me."

The moment the door opened and Jana's eyes met my own, she rushed me, throwing herself into my arms.

"I'm sorry I didn't listen. Fuck, Brycen, I—" her voice broke, and her body surged with tremors. I looked behind me after the door had snicked shut, Jana's boss having left us alone.

"Shhh." My hand drifted to the back of her head, soothingly running down her hair as my other arm cradled her close to me. "I'm here. Whatever it is, I'll handle it."

Her head shook left to right as much as it could, what with her viselike grip on me. "It's not what you think. It's worse. So much worse," she whispered through a hiccup.

"Okay," I whispered, then walked us toward the tiny sofa in the room and guided her to sit next to me, cradling her against my chest. "First, I'm going to look after you. Then, when I'm sure you're a little calmer, I'll see about that parcel. Is that okay, sweetheart?"

She nodded, farther tucking her head under my chin. "I feel like I'm falling apart here."

"Fuck, babe. I'm so sorry this had to happen," I told her. "I've got you."

"Don't let go."

"Wouldn't dream of it."

seven

BRYCEN

"YOU'VE GOT to be fucking kidding me!" Shane swore under his breath as he inspected the box's contents with rubber gloves from a crime kit he kept in his vehicle.

After discovering the haphazardly discarded package on the floor of what Jana and her coworkers called the bullpen—a cheesy term for which they'd dubbed the space where calls were received—I'd immediately called Shane in.

"This motherfucker is one sick fuck," I muttered under my breath because it was still business as usual for all dispatchers, but they were all aware that something was amiss amongst them. "Jana's in one of the quiet rooms, so do what you must, but I need to get back to her."

"I'm on it," Shane shook his head. "How she doing?"

"She's a basket case, but she'll be okay. She has to be."

The man finished putting everything in an evidence box, rose to his full height and studied me. "Be careful, man. I could tell there's something there between you two, but—"

"But nothing, Shane," I told him. "We met before this shit happened, all right? Am I interested, sure. Do I want more? It'll depend on her, but not until this horrorfest is over and done with."

The man nodded in understanding. "Just have the good sense to know if you're in too deep. We're all here for you, Bryce."

I know. "Yeah, thanks."

"Go check on her. Meanwhile, I'll get this to the precinct. I have no fucking doubt this stuff will solidify the partnership between me and the FBI now," Shane grumbled, grabbing the box.

"Keep us posted."

"Like yesterday, right?" His brow was arched in a humorous fashion.

"You know it."

Jana

Just as the memory of those bloody tendrils of hair and scalp threatened to get the best of me, making me one with the room's waste basket, Brycen entered the quiet room.

"You okay?"

Fighting the urge to vomit, I shook my head and stopped almost immediately because the motion made it worse.

"Shane came and went. He collected everything and is sending it all to the lab for analysis as soon as he gets to the precinct. He seems to think that this will solidify their hunch that all three victims are linked."

You think? I thought to myself, but mumbled, "'K," then focused on my breathing.

The man approached, took a seat right next to me, then began to rub my back in gentle circular motions. It soothed some of the nausea away. The heat of his thigh pressed against mine reminded me that I wasn't in this alone either.

"Steve's giving you the rest of the night off." He sighed,

pinching the bridge of his nose. "I think we should get out of here, get you home."

"'K," I repeated my earlier statement.

My gaze fixated beyond my home as Brycen parked his Range Rover. For a split second, I got caught up in worries about what would happen if I had to go into hiding. After all, this guy knew my name, and now which building I worked in, as we have three dispatch offices serving the greater Jacksonville area.

"I'll get your door." Brycen hurried from his seat, then ran across the front of the vehicle to my side of the car.

Escorting me to the front door, he used the key to let us in, deactivating the alarm that had been installed earlier this week, then he reset it.

"You're safe now," he whispered, just as I turned to face him. His arms were open and at the ready, as though he expected me to collapse at any moment.

"I don't feel it," I admitted, taking the one step that brought me toe to toe with him. Without asking for it, I simply took the comfort I knew he was ready to give me. Collapsing into his chest, my hands grabbed the front of his shirt while his arms surrounded me in a tight hold.

"Shane just called," Cade greeted us from the kitchen entranceway. "Jason had to unexpectedly go into work," he explained his sudden presence inside my home. "Everyone okay?"

"I wish you could all stop asking me that," I growled into Brycen's chest. It was solid. Secure. Pure and total comfort, and I was finally feeling able to let go of said comfort to vent. "This has just started and I'm already sick of it. No, I'm not okay. I'm freaking out, dammit, and I'm scared shitless! Why me? Why the fuck *me*?"

Anger may have gotten the better of me, but my burst of

energy was short-lived. So short that once the last of my words left me, I collapsed, darkness enveloping me.

My lids felt as though cement weighed them down, but I managed to slowly take a peek of my surroundings: the softness of the couch, a pillow under my head, a blanket over my legs, and my shoes gone.

"Hey," Brycen whispered as he swiped a strand of hair off my forehead, "you're back."

"What happened?"

"You lost consciousness, sweetheart. I want you to stay where you're lying. I have some hot tea here for you, if you'd like some." Immediately, Brycen produced a cup. "This should help curb those shivers of yours. Here, lift your head a little."

With a hand supporting the back of my neck to aid me in lifting my foggy-minded head, Brycen handed over the mug of tea. Closing my eyes, I savored the sweet apple-like scent of chamomile. "Mmm..." I licked my lips after my first sip.

"Good?"

"Yeah. Can I please sit?"

Brycen grabbed the cup, set it down, and proceeded to help me do just that, keeping me covered with the throw I recognized had come from the couch. As soon as I sat upright, he took a seat next to me, but in the couch's corner, then he handed me the tea again.

"Where's Cade?"

"He left after he made you the tea," Brycen's lips ticked up. "His apology for throwing you over the edge."

"I'm the one who's sorry. I shouldn't have lost it on him."

"You've been through a lot. It's understandable."

"Still, I shouldn't have gone off on him like that."

"Hey." His hand reached out to pinch my chin lightly, turning my head so our eyes connected. "In case you haven't noticed, he's kind of a badass." He smirked, then added a shoulder shrug. "We all are."

I knew my reciprocal smile was strained. "And that means?"

"It means that we can take it."

I could barely stifle the yawn that manifested itself.

"Come here," Brycen lifted his arm and pulled me into his side. "Finish your tea. Then you can get settled for bed, and I'll head outside to my post."

On another yawn, I closed my eyes and mumbled, "Don't go." The last I remember is the light feeling of my mug being taken from my hands, a gentle jarring of our bodies as I presumed Brycen had deposited the cup of warmth he'd provided me to the side, then what felt like the scruff of his face buffing the top of my head as he said, "I've got you. Just sleep."

eight

BRYCEN

CHRIST ON A CRUTCH, she felt perfect in my arms. Her subtle scent of woman and pears was intoxicating, and the warmth of her body against mine was more than enough to lull me into a restless slumber on her sofa. I found myself chasing unseen dangers, thwarting the evils that haunted Jana—things and shadows that threatened her life.

"What the fuck are you doing with my sister?" had me jolting. Had Jana not been mostly on top of me, she'd have been thrown to the floor in my attempt to stand at attention like some prepubescent male getting caught with his virgin hand up his first girlfriend's shirt.

Instead, Jana simply pushed me back into the cushions, slumberous eyes peering down at me, a lazy smile splayed across her lips. Of course, my dick chose that exact moment to make his attraction known, causing my sleepy partner's eyes to go wide with my mortifying realization.

"I asked a question," Jason stressed.

Blushing slightly, Jana was careful about her escape, ensuring she twisted the couch throw enough, so when she'd liberated herself from our current position, my tenting pants remained concealed.

"J-Jace," Jana started, but that's as far as she got.

"Are you fucking kidding me, Matthews?" Jason's eyes glared daggers in my direction. "Should have known you'd try something with—"

Jana didn't allow his words to progress any further. Shooting to her feet, she put a hand against his chest, stopping him from moving toward me. "That's enough!"

The man looked down at his sister, eyebrows furrowed. "That sonofabitch was—"

"What am I, sixteen?" She snorted. Jason took a step back, but she matched his retreat with a step forward. "I get the big brother routine, I do but, Jace, I'm a grown-assed woman." She poked her index finger into his chest. "I can take care of myself." The man turned bright red, and his face morphed into a sheepish expression demonstrating his embarrassment.

"But, sis, he had his hands—" he attempted to no avail.

"Shut up," Jana calmly ordered. "I had a horrible night last night. Brycen was kind enough to stay instead of spending the night outside at his post."

Jason's gaze strayed from his sister's to mine, then back again. The domineering older brother emerged once more. "What. Happened?"

Morning wood well-handled—there was nothing better than a relative walking into a room to quell biological responses —I folded the couch throw, draping it over the back of the piece of furniture, and reallocated the decorative pillows to their former placement before I explained.

"Your sister received a package from that whack job is what happened," I grumbled. "I told her not to open it until either me or one of the guys was there, but—"

Jason's eyes studied his sister, and I could feel his mounting frustration. "But she didn't listen, did she?"

"Got it in one."

Jana sucked her bottom lip between her teeth, a sign I'd discovered that denoted her regret, but also guilt.

"Detective Peters has everything, and it's been sent to the labs for analysis. As it was, it's safe to say your sister was freaked the hell out. I brought her home, but the night's festivities were too much for her." My gaze momentarily trailed to Jana, noting the tension in her shoulders, her eyes narrowing on me as I continued, "She passed out right before Cade left."

"You passed out?" Jason's eyes threw daggers at his kin before his gaze strayed back to mine. "She passed out?"

I gave him a single nod. "Cade helped me get her settled on the couch, then I sent him home."

"And he took care of me, and in my delirium, I fell asleep on top of him. The end! End of story. Nothing more, nothing less," Jana interrupted our back-and-forth with an irritated tone. "You two are talking like I'm not even in the room. I can speak for my fucking self, dammit!"

A smirk spread over my face when Jason's eyes met mine, his expression mirroring mine.

"Oh, Good Lord." She threw her arms up in exasperation. "Save me from overbearing, protective men! It's too early for this bullshit. Who wants coffee?"

"In a thermos, sis," Jason responded as she stormed toward the kitchen. "I'm headed to the gym."

"Humph," came from the kitchen as Jana's banging ensued.

Jason chuckled when I reached for the back of my neck, rubbing the leftover stiffness from our night on the couch, all the while attempting to figure out if Jana was really that upset with us—with me.

"So, tell me, what am I in for if I go in there when you leave?" I asked him.

All humor left his face. "Anything else I should know about

that's going on that my baby sister isn't entirely forthcoming with? In case you didn't know, she's blind when it comes to men and their interest. And I know there's something there." His eyes bored into mine as he said the last words.

My brows furrowed at that statement. "Look—" I started, but Jana stomped back in, shoving a thermos into her brother's hands.

"You're welcome…asshat," she stated, giving me a cursory glance as she turned and headed toward the kitchen once more. "You're still here?" I felt my jaw drop and simply nodded like some hapless idiot.

"Later, Matthews," Jason said as he made his exit, leaving me feeling much like a lamb awaiting slaughter.

The sound of the lock in the front door's tumbler mixed with Jana's heavy sigh. "Coffee's ready," she called out.

I shuffled toward the kitchen, expecting a whole lot of apologizing, because even though she seemed pissed at Jason, I was sure she was at least slightly annoyed with me.

JANA

Damn infuriating men! It's a miracle I could freely fend for myself, what with the abundance of testosterone swirling around me in that living room.

To be honest, I was surprised Brycen had taken over explaining all of what had happened last night. Sure, it took the pressure off me to expound, and I'd have probably butchered things enough that I'd provided far too much information, causing my brother to freak the hell out. No thanks. But as thankful as I was for my protector having been the one to explain, I felt like the ever-delicate flower that would wilt if simply looked at the wrong way. And *that* I couldn't tolerate.

I could speak for myself, and Brycen needed to know this straight out of the gate, unlike my brother. Jason never seemed to clue in. I suppose, had the roles been reversed and he had some psycho after him, I'd be just as diligent in protecting my family as he'd been thus far. It's what we did for one another in this family.

I first heard shuffling of feet, then Brycen's throat cleared. It had taken him all but a minute from the time the front door had been locked with Jason's departure for him to muster up the cojones to face me.

Not bad.

"Look, Jana," he started from behind me. My back was toward the entryway as I sat at one of the island's barstools. "I'm sorry for speaking on your behalf."

Major points! The man knew where he'd gone wrong. Then again, I'd helped him out in that department. *But he didn't have to apologize and did so straightaway.* That said a lot about the kind of man Brycen Matthews was.

Seconds trickled by before I felt more than heard his approach, spotting him from my peripheral. I'd poured him a cup of coffee when I'd readied mine, and it sat in front of one of the empty barstools. I'd left cream, milk, and sugar for him, as I had no idea how he doctored his morning drink.

"Is that for me?" he asked cautiously. I offered him a curt nod. "May I sit?" Another nod.

The man proceeded to mix a hell of a lot more sugar than I'd believed a man of his fitness level would drink with the hot java.

His chuckling had my eyes aiming high up to meet his, and he had that adorable self-deprecating grin on his face again. It had my lips inching upward ever so slightly.

Would you like some coffee with that sugar?

His chuckle turned into a full-blown belly laugh.

Had I said that aloud? My face heated instantly.

"Listen," he said, the feel of his thumb and forefinger under my chin, tilting it upward, forced my gaze to his, "I really am sorry, Jana. I should have let you explain. He's your brother, and I'm sure you know how to handle him a lot better than I can." He took a sip of his coffee, closing his eyes in enjoyment of the brew.

It reminded me of the sleepy-eyed Brycen I'd fallen asleep cuddled against from last night; the same man who'd held and taken care of me to ensure I slept through the night—no nightmares I might add—and the same one I'd felt against the juncture of my thighs upon our rude awakening a mere half hour ago.

"I'm sorry too," I mumbled after a short moment. He'd never know what for, however.

nine

BRYCEN

"SWEETHEART, you've nothing to be sorry about," I told her, capturing her chin with my fingers again, leaning closer to her. "You had every right to be snippy. And I should have known better, coming from a family of women."

Her pupils dilating at my touch and proximity told me she had more than this morning's display of temper on her mind. Her eyes scanned her surroundings, avoiding my gaze, which only confirmed my suspicions.

Her "Breakfast," came out sounding raspy. Jana covered by clearing her throat, then repeating herself. "Would you like some breakfast?"

Smiling, because I was enjoying the fact she seemed as affected by me as I was by her, I said, "Sure. Can I help? I can put something together for us, and you can look after your mom if you'd like. I don't know if she's on a plain diet or if she's eating everything you and Jason are."

. . .

As soon as Jana told her mother I had made breakfast, Eloise decided she had to make an appearance. And that's when Rex arrived.

"There's enough there for you too, Rex," I announced when he walked into the kitchen, visually scanning the space.

As I finished bringing the large breakfast skillet I'd baked over to the table, I turned to find that our latest guest had taken the seat I'd planned on occupying. After a pause that may not have gone unnoticed, what with the humored expression on Eloise's face, I shrugged my shoulders. I then sat between my coworker and Jana's mom, serving the eldest lady first, then her daughter, followed by Rex, then myself. This of course was met with mother and daughter sharing some sort of look, followed by their conspiratorial smiles.

ELOISE

My heavens, that man could cook, and don't get me started on the way I've seen him looking at my daughter. And those manners! If I were another twenty-five or thirty years younger, I'd be drooling over that handsome beach-bum perfection, and in no absolute hurry to get away from certain—or uncertain—danger as it may be.

As Jana's mom, however, I can't help but worry about my youngest child. She and Jason both have sacrificed so much to be able to help me fight this fucking cancer bitch.

If you asked me a year ago if I'd pictured myself today, living as I am now, I can't say that I would have. If only I could have been stronger, then maybe I'd leave this earth with some semblance of more than simply two amazing kids in this world.

I don't begrudge my life decisions. I've lived plenty, laughed to my heart's content, and done my fair share of crying—and not all the bad kind. But where I lacked was the wherewithal to pursue my one life's regret...finding a man to be there for my children, to show them how life could have been enhanced by a good and constant man in their lives.

Jana has that now, I tell myself, but I know it not to be the case. Not yet anyway.

Oh, my little girl is quite the pessimist when it comes to love, and she carries the largest unsavory chip on her shoulder about relationships. It's not her fault; she'd had her fair share of disappointments in life too. But it was also high time for her to get over herself and her long list of reservations that led to her being so standoffish.

"This is delicious, Brycen," I said, clearing the last bite from my plate.

"Yeah, man, where the hell—" Rex's eyes bugged out and he looked apologetically to a giggling Jana first, then me. "Sorry, ma'am. What I meant to say is, where did you learn to cook like that?"

"When you come from a large family, most of which are of the female persuasion, learning how to cook kind of comes as a package deal," Brycen explained, grinning. "Mom used to say, 'I'll be damned if I send my one and only son out into the world not knowing how to fend for himself or his family.'" I smiled at the fondness and love lacing his words. "Then again, Dad did most of the cooking at home, so I grew up thinking it was a manly thing to do."

Jana smiled sweetly. "That's cute."

Brycen shrugged a shoulder, a subtle blush spreading over his cheeks. "I have to admit, I don't cook nearly enough now that I'm on my own. With my work schedule as it is, my drawer of take-out menus is overused and overflowing."

"Amen," Rex seconded his colleague's words, toasting the man with his coffee mug. "Matthews here, is usually the first to mooch someone's leftovers at the office."

Brycen gave his coworker a warning glare that had me laughing.

"Well, I think it's a beautiful memory, Brycen." I patted the top of his hand, smiling at him. "I'm sure your parents are proud of the man you've become. And I can relate mooching food off others. I do it every day now," I added, throwing him a teasing wink.

The most adorable blush spread from his cheeks to the tips of his ears, giving me the urge to giggle. So I let loose.

Jana

Hearing Mom's tinkling laugh had me smiling at Brycen. It was a sound I hadn't heard from her in far too long, and I could kiss him for giving me a gift he was unaware of gracing me with.

Truth be told, Jason, Mom, and I have been in the dumps lately because of her most recent test results. Add in the fact I have some deranged murderer first calling, and now, sending me bits and pieces of his victims—at work no less—and it's been damn hard to find happiness, humor, or even smile as of late.

Sure, Brycen had made life a little brighter and lighter since having met him, but I never expected him to do the same for my family.

Hell, he'd gotten my mother to grace us with her presence around the dining room table for breakfast when normally she would stay in bed, picking at bits and pieces of her food through most of the morning before calling it quits, leaving my brother and me to exchange the stale dish with her lunch tray. Rinse and repeat—every damn day.

I missed the days when Mom would surprise us at our respective homes with some home-cooked concoction she'd discovered either on TV or online. I craved to have her vivaciousness back, the way she would smile like she was always up to something, and her laugh...because she simply truly enjoyed everything, and most of all, everyone around her.

In its place now, she reminisced about the *old* days, the

antics we'd get up to as a family, or even as individuals. She was constantly stuck in the past, reliving memories instead of forging ahead, making new ones.

It was as if she'd given up with the doctor's latest news.

As Rex helped with settling Mom in her bedroom—after she shooed me away—I went to check on what Brycen was up to in the kitchen. I found him drying his hands, shutting the dishwasher door, no dirty dishes to be seen, and the kitchen was spotless.

Before I knew it, I'd walked straight up to the man and planted my lips against his cheek as soon as he'd turned, reveling in the surprised yet soft expression that covered his face.

"What was that for?" His voice had dropped a few octaves.

"Thank you," I answered shyly.

"Had to eat, right?" he explained.

"Yeah, but you didn't have to—"

Brycen's finger over my lips halted my words. "Don't mention it. I just thought your mom and you could use a good home-cooked meal. If some good cooking helps get your mother out of that room of hers, enjoying company, and smiling, then I'm happy. If I'm being honest, you look exhausted, so I did it mostly for—"

Grasping his hand lightly, I pulled it away, then leaned forward, shutting him up with my lips.

It was a small press, but I hoped it conveyed how appreciative I truly was. He'd managed things Jason and I hadn't been able to in too long.

Pulling away, I couldn't help but feel the erratic puffs of Brycen's breath over my mouth, and I wanted nothing more than to explore his sweetness, but I craved his arms more. In hopes I wouldn't have to explain that last kiss, I simply allowed myself the luxury of hugging a now mute Brycen around the waist. After a fraction of a second, his arms surrounded me tightly, his scruffy cheek buffing the top of my head.

When was the last time I'd been able to simply relax in someone's arms, feeling safe and sheltered, and unafraid of being hurt?

Barring family? Never.

ten

BRYCEN

IT WAS JUST A THANK-YOU PECK, *nothing to write home about,* I reminded myself for the umpteenth time today.

After that kiss, I'd had to make my way into the office, leaving Rex in charge of Jana and her mother when all I'd wanted to do was hold her longer, tilting her head up to mine, ravishing her mouth the way I'd been craving.

"Woohoo! Did you hear me?" Devolin's waving hand in front of my face snapped me back to reality.

I shook my head, focusing on my boss's wife. "Huh?"

"Oh shit, I think you've really got it bad, Baby—"

"Shut up," I said without much malice. "What was it you were saying?"

"The First Bank datacenter case is officially closed and paid out," she announced. "I just thought I'd let you know since you thought you'd fucked up that op." I nodded. "Dalton said they're in the process of negotiating a new contract with us now."

"Really?" I guess I hadn't read Mayer all that well. Then

again, I hadn't spoken to the man with the exception of the time I'd called him at stupid o'clock. "That's fantastic news."

Devolin's head bobbed up and down, and I could tell she was eager to learn things.

"Just ask, Huss." I laughed lightly, using the moniker we'd all grown to know during an op-gone-bad, which felt like ages ago.

"What's going on with that Elway case?" she blurted out. "You gonna go for it with Jana, or you going to just sit in this office and stew over your undeniable attraction toward the woman?"

"How about I let you in on everything when I know myself," I told her.

Her brows furrowed. "Everything okay?"

"I dunno," I said, shaking my head. "I feel like I'm missing something in all of this, but I don't know Jana well enough to pinpoint what it is yet. If you're asking me about instant attraction, yeah, it's there in spades. She seems to be standoffish, and honestly, part of me appreciates the distance she puts between us, because I'm better able to work at keeping her safe."

"But it's confusing, right?" Devolin had hit the proverbial nail on the head.

"Yeah."

"And Kip tells me that a few of the guys have warned you off her, at least until we know more about who this sicko is," she added.

Had it truly come to this? Were my coworkers so bored outside of work affairs that they'd taken up gossiping like old schoolmarms in the lunchroom?

"You'd be right on that," I said.

"So, naturally, you want what you shouldn't have; am I right?" she surmised aloud. "It's a typical human reaction, Bryce. We all go through it at some point or another."

"But it has nothing to do with why I'm attracted to her," I explained.

"Then, if you want my opinion, just go for it," Dev plainly stated, then looked past my shoulder. "Right, Ember?"

Emberlyn walked into our tech hub at that moment, a large grin on her face. "If you two are talking about that 9-1-1 dispatcher the guys are yapping about in the conference room, then yeah, Bryce, go for it. By the way, they need you both for an update on that case. I'm going to head out. I have some errands to run before I pick up the car from the shop. Shane drove me in," she explained.

Devolin hugged our friend before hightailing it to the conference room, and Emberlyn stopped my forward progress with a gentle touch to my arm.

Her eyes were gentle and caring. "Seriously, just do it. If anyone will understand that pull you feel, it'll be Shane. Never mind what my husband told you."

I nodded. "Thanks."

"And when something finally happens between you two, I expect a dinner date." With a wink, she made her way to the reception area of our office suite, and moments later, I heard the telltale click of the door's latch snick closed.

Jana

Mom had spent the better part of the day in bed, sleeping, which had left me with loads of time to tackle a few house projects I hadn't gotten around to finishing, especially the decluttering and organizing of the kitchen cabinets after both she and Jason had moved in.

Believe me, I was more than grateful all Brycen had needed was a deep CorningWare dish, a few knives, a spatula, and regular table utensils for his breakfast concoction, or else, there'd have been a disaster of epic proportions in the form of a dish tsunami tumbling out onto my face.

So, there I was, sitting in the middle of my kitchen floor,

sifting through the oodles of food storage containers I'd amassed over the last few months when I heard footsteps.

"Jana?"

"Right here, Rex," I called out, waving a white plastic top, hoping maybe he'd come to rescue me from what felt like an unsurmountable disaster. Okay, so I was being a little dramatic, but you should have seen it. If I'd had the disposable income, I'd have certainly thrown it all away and gone on a shopping spree to buy only the containers that were most useful. Instead, I'd invested in a multitude of storage containers, bins, and organizers to hopefully ensure the Tupperware cabinet would never get out of hand like that again.

Seriously, what's with using containers to contain other containers?

"What in the hell?" he blurted out while leaning over the edge of the island countertop to find me swimming in storage solutions.

"Since I'm not going in to work tonight, I figured I'd tackle a small project," I explained.

The man guffawed. "You call this *small*? Looks more like a mountain right now, hon. Just dropping the mail. Where did you want it?"

"The island is good," I answered. Before I knew it, Rex had gone back to his post, leaving me to make some sense out of my kitchen chaos.

By dinnertime, Jason had arrived home only to shower and change.

"Got a date," he muttered before I heard the beeping of security alarm buttons, and the front door opening, then closing, and locks...

The locks never engaged.

Instead, the door opened and shut again.

"Forget something?" I called out from the couch in the living room.

"Not unless you wanted Dr. Pepper instead of Pepsi." Brycen had me jumping out of my skin as he appeared in the living room entrance with a large pizza, a six-pack of light beer—*is that Bud Light?*—and another of Pepsi.

"You scared the crap out of me," I said breathlessly, a hand on my chest.

"Would you get the alarm, and lock the door? Your brother seemed in too much of a hurry when I got here, so I told him I'd handle it."

I immediately got to my feet to do just that as Brycen headed for the kitchen, where I joined him as soon as I had done what he'd instructed.

"What're you doing here, I thought shift change isn't for another hour?" I asked at the same time Brycen said, "What the hell happened here?"

Pausing to look around, I blushed at the mess of leftover storage solutions that littered the far corner of the kitchen by the back patio door while Brycen set food and drink down on the island countertop.

I'd given up on my kitchen organization nightmare after three hours of pulling stuff out, washing the cupboards, then stuffing everything in a new tidy place. I'd only managed to get half done. Yeah, not a small undertaking in the least.

"I should have tackled things as those storage containers arrived," was my explanation.

"Pardon?"

"When you made breakfast this morning, I spent most of the time hoping you wouldn't need too much in the way of dishes." My face heated. "Let's just say that things are a bit cluttered since Mom and Jace moved in, and opening some cabinetry in here has become a bit like a game of whack-a-mole, wondering when something will topple out and which toe it'll land on."

Brycen's expression was one of curiosity, bewilderment, and humor before he roared with laughter. Meanwhile, I found myself unable to do more than admire the sheer look of entertainment on his face, and delight in the man's laughter. He was honest in his expressions, deliberate in his actions, and sincere with his words.

I could get used to that.

"Sweetheart, I have to say there's never a dull moment with you," he professed as he turned to grab plates from the cabinet I'd fetched them from this morning. "How about this…" He paused, studying me. "After we feed your mother, and ourselves, I'll help you finish this"—his arms gestured toward the entire kitchen space—"organizing project of yours. Then, we can sit down, and I can give you a progress report on your case. After that, we'll set a movie up, then it'll be off to an early bedtime for you."

I was speechless.

Moving slowly, Brycen left the dishes and our food to approach me. He slipped his index under my chin and lifted.

"To answer your question, I'm here because I want to be," he explained, his voice soft. "Tate's got shift tonight, starting in about an hour or so, so this is more like me being a friend, ensuring that you're taken care of and helping out any way I can."

Friend. Sure.

The thoughts that ran through my mind right then had everything to do with how we woke up, fast-forwarding to that kiss I'd spent the better part of the day wishing I'd deepened, and every damn daydream I've had on and off since I'd met him.

And they were definitely not *friendly* thoughts in the way he was alluding to.

eleven

Brycen

"SO WHO'S TATE?" she asked, a beer in one hand, her nearly decimated first slice of pizza in the other.

"He's one of our full-timers," I explained, dropping a second slice of pizza onto my plate. I'd made enough room for us at the kitchen island while Jana had looked in on her mother, who'd kindly refused dinner. "He just got back from a few months' leave, which is why you haven't met him. He'll probably pop in to introduce himself when he gets here to trade places with Rex."

"Mmm," she answered around the last bite of her slice, reaching for another from the pizza box between us. "So tell me, since I'm not working, anything new with your job?"

"Already have no idea what to do with yourself, I see." I smirked over the bottle of beer at my mouth. Taking a leisurely sip, I proceeded, "Is that why this whole kitchen thing has come about?"

She blushed the most endearing shade of pink. "Maybe," she answered in a singsong fashion before taking a bite of her second slice. "Seriously, though," she added after swallowing her food, "I want to know about your day."

"Not much to tell, really," I answered, shrugging my shoulders. "D negotiated a new contract with a client I've been supporting. We briefed Tate in on your case, so now we don't have to work Rex, Shane, or Cade as much." The guilty look on Jana's face had me backpedaling. "No, no, no! It's not just your case. The guys have been burning the candle at both ends lately between NSI growing, and D, Shane, and I stalling on making decisions on some new staff."

"Shane?" she asked.

"He's a majority owner, like I am, but hasn't managed to leave the JPD yet," I explained. "D's been trying to steal him away since shit hit the fan with Devolin, and then there was that kidnapping thing with Emberlyn last year—"

Jana's eyes widened in shock. "What?"

"Mm-hmm." I nodded. "I never told you the guys at NSI have a knack of finding their women whenever their lives go down the crapper, did I?"

Her mouth dropped open, pizza at the ready, but never quite making it to its final destination. "For real?"

"Uh, yeah." I explained, then listed everything that's gone on with some of my colleagues and friends: Theo and Morgan Lowell—not to mention his nephew—then there had been D and Huss's ordeal, then there was Shane and Ember, and more recently, there'd been Cade and Aspen. *Now me...* my subconscious added, but I kept that to myself, along with the growing fluttering warmth in my belly.

Jana's eyes never left mine as I recounted the CliffsNotes version of what had gone down with each couple, her gaze round, expression one of disbelief, and her half-eaten pizza slice had flopped to her plate, forgotten.

Finally, when all was said and done, the woman seemed in deep thought, her brows having furrowed while she focused on peeling the sweaty label off her now empty beer bottle. I got up to fetch us a second drink.

"My situation seems to pale in comparison," she blurted, causing me to look at her—really *look* at her—and assess where her head might be at with all that's been going on with her lately.

Taking my seat, I popped the top off one bottle, then handed it to her. Jana took a large sip from it as soon as her fingers had wrapped themselves around the brown glass.

"I wouldn't say that at all, sweetheart," I told her, opening my own bottle. "Every situation was different, with its own set of circumstances. But don't kid yourself, every single one of those women have stared death in the face. Your case isn't any different, or have you forgotten you're on a serial killer's list of contacts?"

JANA

Well, when he worded it that way...

"I hadn't thought of that," I mumbled, picking at a piece of pepperoni on my partially forgotten slice of what had started as the best pizza I'd ever eaten. "Three makes a serial killer, right, or has that changed? I'm sure I'm not all up on that criminology craft you guys are used to."

Brycen shook his head. "No, you're right about the three," he said in a disgusted manner, "but serial or not, three victims or thirty, it doesn't discount the threat to you. As much as I hate it, that's still very much real, babe."

No, it didn't discount anything in the least. I was still freaked out at how I'd managed to get on this sicko's radar at all. Choosing to ignore his *babe* moniker, I led with the next logical question, even though it wasn't quite time for that part of Brycen's well-thought-out plans for the evening.

"Since we're talking about it, why don't we just skip to if there've been any new discoveries regarding my case."

His eyes darkened, the edges of his mouth tightening. "You sure you don't want to finish dinner first? You seemed famished earlier, and I can't help but notice you're now only picking at—"

"I'll keep eating," I promised. He'd had me forgetting about my appetite earlier, simply because the stories he told me about his friends were like something you'd find in some suspense book—I'd been enthralled.

The man stared at me as if he awaited proof that I would live up to my word.

Grabbing my slice of pizza, I took a much-too-large bite from it, uttering, "See?" right before stretchy cheese slipped off, slopping onto my chin.

Despite the embarrassment I felt, my goof had netted me with one of the man's belly laughs. I enjoyed the sound so wholeheartedly, it had become contagious, and I couldn't help but join in as I mopped at my face, making sure I got the saucy cheese mix with my napkin.

Hilarity of the moment having passed, Brycen's face sobered. "Let's make a deal. I love a woman who isn't apologetic about the way she eats. So, as long as you keep eating, I'll keep talking."

On a single nod, I added, "Deal." For good measure, I took a much daintier bite of my slice of pizza, trying to salvage whatever remained of my proper womanly image, even though certain said image had gone out the window about a few hours after I'd first met this man.

The edges of Brycen's mouth ticked up slightly, for all too short of a moment, before his expression faded into a somber one. "Right, okay... The preliminary results came back from the coroner, confirming that all three hair and tissue samples you received belong to each victim."

"Okay." I grabbed my beer bottle and took a large gulp. "We

figured that was going to be the case. Any leads on who this guy is?"

"That's the other part. The box, wrapping, even the tape are still being analyzed. Nothing's come from those yet," he answered.

Then what else is there? "You do still think this is a guy, right?"

"It's what Shane, the JPD, and the FBI seem to think, and considering his targets have all been female, I'm tending to side with that assumption," he stated, taking a bite of a third slice of pizza he'd just pulled from the box. "Shane and his partner are looking into seeing if there's anything that connects these women, yourself included. Nothing to report on that yet, but our electronic portion of the investigation is something that takes time, so I'm not surprised. Devolin and I are looking into every electronic trail to make sure we cover all areas of their personal lives." I nodded in understanding that I'd be investigated too if they hadn't already. The man's eyes met mine. "I can't have anyone miss anything, Jana. Not when there's something I can do to help. Not when—"

My hand reached out to clasp Brycen's forearm, stalling his reach for his drink. His eyes diverted from mine to my hand. The muscles beneath my fingers twitched, and I couldn't help but to allow my thumb to rub the taut bronzed skin, even though I'd convinced myself it was simply an appeasement gesture to calm the man before me, who seemed nervous all of a sudden.

"Brycen?"

"Hmm," he managed before he covered my hand with his.

I swallowed hard, my eyes trailing back up to his. Once our gazes met, they stuck, and I felt my mouth go dry.

"Thank you," I whispered, feeling my body start to lean in toward him, his Adam's apple bobbing as he swallowed; his demeanor having gone from serious, to nervous, to sweet, then downright smoldering in the span of seconds.

"Ja—" Brycen was cut off by a key in the front door's tumbler. I watched as the haze of lust disappeared, almost as if it had never been there, and the relaxed persona he'd had moments before had vanished, transforming into one of business. Keeping hold of my hand as he lifted it off his forearm, he said, "Shift change. That's probably Tate or Rex checking in. How 'bout you put the rest of this food away, and if it's Tate, once we're done with the introductions, you and I can tackle that disastrous abundance of storage you've got left over?"

Without preamble, he squeezed the hand he still held, got to his feet, then released me. Having stood up to do as he'd suggested, my back was to the kitchen's exit, when "Oh, and Jana," came.

Peering over my shoulder, I asked, "Yeah?"

I was met by a grin that showed off the man's dimples. "Don't think I'll forget about what was about to happen, sweetheart," he stated. Without waiting for a response, he left me standing speechless, our plates in one hand, pizza box in the other.

Well...

twelve

Jana

SPICES! *Now where did I go and put that fucking spice rack?* I asked myself while going through piles of bags and boxes stacked in my kitchen.

After putting away our dinner, leaving our unfinished beers on the counter to drink while I got things sorted for what Brycen and I could tackle in the kitchen, I had opted to kill some time—and distract myself from our almost kiss—with transferring some spices into this new wall mountable spice rack I'd purchased. But damn if I could find it.

Bent over in half, ass up in the air, I cursed. "Where the fuck are yo—"

My words faltered as I spotted the box that held the rack and bottles, and I simultaneously heard, "Uhm, Jana?"

"Huh?" I asked, turning to peer at where Brycen's voice had come from and was met with two sets of eyes filled with humor. *Shit!* Taking into account the position I was in, I set the box down, and straightened to my full height. On a deep breath, collecting my humiliated self, I turned, then proceeded toward them, my hand outstretched, leading with, "You must be Tate."

Smirking, his eyes held mine. "And you must be Janice Elway."

"Jana's fine," I responded, his big hand enveloping mine entirely. *Wow! Was it a requirement to be sexy as hell to work for NSI or something?*

Tate's man-bunned head tilted back and he roared with laughter as Brycen added, "Or something, I'd say," before he joined him.

Oh my! "Please excuse my brain. Apparently, it missed today's memo that not all thoughts should be spoken aloud. I blame it on Brycen, the beer, and the fact my mind hasn't been challenged by work today." I shrugged my shoulders, giving our new arrival a self-deprecating smile.

As soon as Tate released my hand, Brycen came to stand at my side.

"Rex left?" The man gave him a single nod in response. "Good. While you're on, keep me in the loop if anything looks or feels off," he told him. "We don't know if this fucker knows where she lives, but he sure as fuck knows where she works."

Tate had the tough-guy single nod down pat. "Anything else?"

"Nothing's changed since we filled you in on where we're at."

The man's demeanor transformed to something scary, "Yeah, let's hope answers start coming soon." His gaze set itself on me. "If you need anything, Little Lady, day or night, just holler." Could his Texas drawl come out any thicker?

"O-okay," I whispered.

Brycen wrapped an arm around my shoulders, tucking me into his side. Tate didn't pay attention to the gesture, his subtle quirk of a lip being the only giveaway to him noticing his co-worker's move.

"Mean it, Jana." The man's imposing gaze kept mine trapped. "Day or night."

Gulping down my apprehension, all I could do was nod. Just as soon as I did, Tate graced me with another one of those manly curt nods, turned on his heel and headed to the front of the house. After pushing a few buttons to arm the security system, he let himself out of the house, then the tumbler clicked to indicate I was once again locked into safety mode.

Brycen

"Jeeze! Does everyone who works for NSI have the *if I look at you the right way, you'd be dead* look?" she jabbered on, turning away from me, then headed back to the pile of boxes. Picking one of them up, she set it on the kitchen island and started removing what looked like small glass bottles with stainless steel lids. "What is up with you giants? And seriously," she paused to look at me, unseeingly, "are good looks a prerequisite? I mean, I know Rex has a few scars, and I thought he was scary until Tate just now, but there's something about Rex, you know?" Setting the last of the bottles on the counter, she turned for a cabinet where I spotted heaps of spices—bottles, shakers, bags—and she kept on going. "Who'd have thought it would take a bloody serial killer for a bevy of hot men to come knocking at my door?" She proceeded to scatter every package from her cabinets onto the island countertop. "Mom is having a field day trying to pick which one of you to marry me off to before she dies, by the way." Stopping dead in her tracks, she dropped the last of the packages, her eyes beginning to water the moment she realized what she'd just said.

Oh, fuck! The waterworks were coming fast and furious, and it pained me to watch her suffer while keeping my distance, because I was fighting a bout of petty jealousy that had reared its ugly head around the time she started spouting stuff about my coworkers' looks. "Shit, Jana." My words were pained. It wasn't like me to not offer comfort, and despite my hang-ups—or maybe to spite them—I took the necessary steps toward her, and pulled her into my chest.

"I don't know why I said that," she cried, her body shaking like a leaf as she struggled to keep her emotions in check.

"Sweetheart," I said, kissing the crown of her hair, then squeezed her tight on a sigh after she'd wrapped her arms around my middle. "I've got you."

Her nails dug into the back of my shirt, pulling me to her. "I'm sorry I even said it," she hiccupped. "I-I…"

"Let it out," I told her, "I'm not letting go." *I can't*, was left unsaid.

Spotting movement from the corner of my eye, I shifted my gaze to find Eloise standing in the kitchen's entryway, taking the scene in with subtle trepidation in her expression.

Eloise

I watched as Brycen held fast to my daughter, and I *knew*. I knew she'd found the home she'd been destined to. I felt, with every fiber of my being, that the man who'd made us all breakfast this morning, only because he'd thought Jana looked tired, would be the glue who would keep us all together, even if I met my demise. Oh, my daughter was in trouble, and by the unapologetic look of sadness mixed with so many emotions in that man's gaze as it connected with mine, if she didn't know about his intentions yet—or even suspected them—she'd be in the know soon. I just prayed I'd be around long enough to see how it played out.

When Brycen crooked a small finger to get me to come closer, I shored my shoulders and made my approach.

"What's all this?" I cooed, setting a hand on Jana's shoulder.

"M-mama?" she hiccupped, then turned to take me in her arms, cuddling her head into the crook of my neck.

I held her fast and steady, my eyes burning at the strength of her emotions. Brycen made to take a step back, but I shook my head once, just as Jana's hand reached out to clutch at the front of his shirt. The man offered us his silent support, allowing for my daughter to keep a single hand on him as he laid one upon my shoulder.

Calm. Steady. *Strong.*

"Now, now, baby girl, why don't you tell me what these tears are all about," I coaxed, knowing all too well the excitement of the past couple of weeks had reached its peak with her and was finally boiling over.

By the time I'd gotten Jana to spill the beans as to her current state of mind, my daughter had curled up alongside me in the bedroom she'd set up for me when I moved in.

Brycen had left us alone a little over an hour ago, allowing us time to talk, cry some more, stating he was just a holler away if needed, and if not, he'd be back to check on us anyway.

When the man made his reappearance, our eyes connected briefly before his soft gaze fell upon the exhausted and unconscious heap of my daughter and held there. He looked like a man who wanted. Pained. Confused. Undecided, yet strong in his convictions. He also looked as if he wanted to say something but was at an impasse.

Instead, he approached slowly, and sat in the reading chair that had been pulled closer to my bed so on my bad days, I could have a seat on something sturdier than a mattress to dress myself. After all, I still had my dignity to preserve, and if I could, I'd stretch that small luxury for as long as possible.

Leaning forward, his elbows on his knees, his heart in his eyes, he sighed, scrubbing at his face.

"Don't sound so defeated," I told him. As soon as his eyes met mine, I added, "She'll see what's been there all along, eventually." Smiling, I extended my only free hand to him, not at all surprised when he took it in both of his immediately.

"How is she?" he rasped quietly so as not to wake her.

I shrugged, the guilt on how much I was reliant on her—Jason too—weighing heavily. "A wreck. I was wondering when she'd break."

His hands gave mine a tender squeeze before he asked, "And how are you?"

"I'm as okay as I can be, Brycen." I smiled sadly then looked to Jana, who was latched to my other hand, having pulled it to her chest. "She used to do this whenever she'd wake in the middle of the night from a nightmare," I explained. "Very tactile this one. Just a simple touch calms her. It's something you should remember for—"

"Eloise," he interrupted my train of thought, shaking his head.

"No," I argued, tightening my hold on the hand of his that met my palm. "I'm not talking about when my time comes, Son," I assured him. His relieved expression was palpable. "Honey, I've seen the way you look at her. It's beyond simple interest."

"It is," he admitted. "Regardless—"

"Oh, don't you dare give me this whole *it's not the right time* bullshit, Brycen Matthews," I argued. "Jana's told me about how you two met." His eyes widened rather comically. "She's never been one to have faith in relationships, probably because of what she's been through, and what she's witnessed between her father and me. It's my fault she never believed in finding happiness with a partner. By the time I'd clued in to her rebellion against commitment, I was afraid I was too late. Now I know otherwise."

"So, what you're saying is?" he urged me to go on.

"What I'm saying is, you might have to knock her over the head with one of those crazy storage solution boxes littering the kitchen, or maybe something sturdier, but she'll eventually come to see the truth." I paused, leaning my head against the headboard and closing my eyes, feeling the potential of witnessing her joy warming me from the inside out. After a short moment of basking in the feeling, I opened my eyes once more, focusing on the man sitting across from me. "Whether you've realized it or not"—I nod my head to indicate Jana—"my daughter trusts you completely. She's already in deeper than I've ever seen her with others. Letting you into her—into *our*—lives was a massive step for her. Giving of her true self, unafraid of showing emotion, that's more proof."

Brycen's brows furrowed before he said, "She trusts all of us, it's not just me. Eloise—"

"Has she been crying all over Rex? How 'bout her brother? Or what's his name…oh, that's right…Cade, or how about that Dalton fellow or any of the others who come and go?" He shook his head hesitantly in answer but seemed to keep analyzing my words. "No?" I inquired as to his answer.

"N-no, ma'am," he all but choked out. "We might have met before shit hit the fan, pardon my French, but she thinks this is nothing but a job for me at this point."

"I highly doubt that, but you too will come to see," I all but guaranteed. "Now come here." I pulled him closer by his hands. "She needs her bed just as much as I need to settle for the night. I don't have the heart to wake her, and—"

"And you're enjoying her closeness so much that you're willing to suffer through a night of little to no sleep just to have Jana at your side," he surmised.

Pulling my hand from his, I smiled, then patted his cheek. "Smart man."

Brycen grinned. "Do you need anything before I take care of our girl, here?"

Checking that my glass of water was filled, and my pills were where they always were on my nightstand, I gave the man a tired smile and shook my head. "I'm good here."

Leaning farther forward, having gotten to his feet, Brycen

gently tilted my head forward, depositing the sweetest kiss to the crown of my head. "Get some rest. I'll be checking on you later."

thirteen

BRYCEN

THE MOMENT I'd entered the sanctuary of Jana's bedroom, I never wanted to leave. The deep bluish indigo of her walls was offset by light blues and purples in her bedding, mixed with some gray accent pieces of furniture like the chaise lounge by her bedroom window, which I presumed she used to read in, judging by the piled books accompanied by an e-reader on the side table next to it.

Beyond that, her scent was everywhere, and it drove my libido into a tailspin.

Not now, creeper. Just put her to bed and get the fuck out.

Approaching her bed, I bent to lower her to her mattress, but when I made to let her go, Jana nuzzled into my neck and only tightened her hold.

"Stay," she whispered in slumber.

"I wouldn't dream of leaving," I whispered back, thinking she'd finally let go, and I'd be able to maybe tackle a few more things for her in the kitchen, or simply leave it be for the night, settling on the couch long enough for me to fall into slumber—crick in the neck be damned.

"No, stay," she said with a bit more conviction to her words. "Bed...with me."

Fuck, she was killing me. So sweet and innocent had been her request, yet my dick thought it was an opportune time to fly its freak flag at full mast.

Looking toward the door, feeling torn between being honorable on a couch made for shorties, or doing so in a large comfy bed with her warm body next to mine, I chose the latter.

"Okay, sweetheart, but we need to get you under these covers," I told her.

Once she'd let go of me, I went to work, pulling back the blankets from one side of the bed, then repositioning her. Heading to the side closest to the door, I emptied my pockets onto her dresser, removed my socks and belt, stopping there. Getting into Jana's bed, alongside her, I settled onto my side, facing the woman who'd been at the forefront of my mind since we'd met.

It wasn't until I felt Jana move in closer, where the crown of her head snuggled against my chin, did I fade into slumber.

JANA

So hot. Why is it so fucking hot? I wondered to myself.

As I slowly became aware of my surroundings, I could feel the warmth of a body snuggled the length of the back of mine, but I instinctively knew who it was, and I melted.

He stayed.

Yes, I remembered having made that request when he'd been so sweet the night before to carry me to my bed instead of waking me. And instinctively, I knew he'd ensured Mom had been taken care of before taking care of me. It was just the type of man Brycen Matthews was.

Refusing to give in to full wakefulness—I wanted to relish in the sensation of being wrapped in his arms, if only for a little while longer—I made to snuggle backward, impossibly closer to my bedmate.

It wasn't until I heard the man groan, then thrust gently against my ass that I realized what I'd done.

Arms tightened around my torso, bringing me close enough that air couldn't pass between Brycen and me before he spoke.

"Don't. Move."

The sound of his sleep-roughened voice had me shivering, and I subconsciously rubbed my legs together to quell the heat building between my thighs.

This can't be happening.

But it was.

"Fu-uck," he groaned, "I said, don't move." He delivered a brief kiss to the back of my shoulder, making me realize that the contact had been skin to skin.

It wasn't until Brycen's teeth grazed the skin he'd gently pressed his lips to that I began to wonder how in the hell I had ended up topless.

Not shirtless.

Not in a bra and underwear, and I knew the latter were still on. *Thank God!*

Topless!

As soon as my faculties were on an even keel, that's when my body went rigid.

"Relax, sweetheart," he rumbled into the back of my neck. "I didn't see anything." He groaned as I melted into him, despite my apprehension. "And I haven't touched anything," came out in a growl that told me it had taken a hell of a lot of self-restraint on his part to keep his large hands off me.

The warm palm that held me fast to him started to slide away and I found myself instantly dreading the pending loss of his heat—the feel of him.

"No, don't," I whispered, biting my bottom lip to evade the moan that wanted to creep up. "I-I—"

"You must have stripped during the night," he explained,

staying where he was. "I swear, we went to sleep with all our clothes on. But I'm not going to say I regret this predicament we're in, sweetheart." Another graze of his teeth over my shoulder had me shuddering. "Ever since that first night, when you told me you slept in the buff, I've wondered what it would be like to hold you just like this."

"Please tell me you're not naked," I blurted softly.

"No." He paused, then chuckled. "I got up around two this morning and went to check on your mom. I put a call in with Tate to make sure all was good." The hand that held me to him began a soothing tickle over my abdomen. "I came back and stripped down to my underwear because, babe, you're a veritable furnace when you're knocked out." I couldn't help the short giggle that escaped. "I didn't realize, until after I'd snuck back under the covers, and you burrowed against me, that somehow, your clothes had disappeared in the time I'd left your room."

"Well, that explains it," I mumbled, then made to roll over to my back, ensuring that sheets stayed tucked around my bare boobs.

Brycen shifted to give me the necessary room, his palm never leaving my midsection while it left a path of heat in its wake as it traveled to my waist.

My pulse skyrocketed the moment our eyes met. Spotting Brycen's throat undulating as he swallowed, it was clear I wasn't the only one affected.

Sporting a shy grin, I led with, "Good morning."

Dark brown eyes deepened to rich dark chocolate pools as the man rested his head in the hand of his opposite arm, propping him just so he hovered slightly above me. Smirking, he rumbled, "Good morning, indeed." Expression sobering, albeit tinted with subtle nuances of concern, he added, "How'd you sleep?"

Refusing to give in to the despair I'd felt last night, I uttered a simple, "Better than okay," and lifted a hand to touch the chest on display before me like my fingers itched to do.

Brycen's breath hitched as my skin made contact with the taut golden expanse of his.

Yeah, he was definitely as affected by this turn of events as I was.

The man's eyes closed, and his face warred with notes of pain and enjoyment. When his lids lifted, an untamed wildfire could be seen in his irises, and I knew things had not only shifted, but they'd changed entirely.

BRYCEN

Chivalry died the moment her tiny hand smoothed over my chest. It wasn't an attempt to be sexy or provocative. Hell, it hadn't been what I would consider an inviting gesture, but every notion in me to keep things simple between us went out the proverbial window.

"Jana," I warned, squeezing my hand at her hip, attempting to read her eyes. When her tongue escaped to moisten her lips, my brain fizzled out. "Fuck it."

Slamming my mouth to hers, I plundered, and I pillaged what she was willing to give.

Fingers feathered aggressively through the hair at the back of my head, and Jana offered me a moan, which I inhaled. The simple taste of the skin on her shoulder upon waking had done nothing to glean what the dark sweetness of her mouth and tongue would hold. And tasting her then still felt like it wasn't enough. It wouldn't be until I'd tasted *all* of her.

That's why I slowed things down, pulling away slowly before we did something we'd both regret.

Dropping my forehead to her shoulder, I attempted to breathe away the urge to consume her.

"Brycen," Jana panted, "did I— Did I do something wrong?"

On a huffed laugh, I quelled her worries. "Shit, woman, you do everything right." I lifted my head so our eyes connected. "That's part of the problem. *My* problem, not yours, sweetheart." Her furrowed brows had me spilling more. "Babe." I pressed a chaste kiss to her lips. "I'm trying to be patient, professional, and a friend all at once. I'm not sure it's wise to be more than that right now. Something tells me you're not ready for it, with all that's happening."

JANA

Ever been told you couldn't have something and claimed to accept it? It always led to craving it more, didn't it? Even when it was the most rational conclusion.

Well, that's where I was.

Talk about being stuck between a rock and a hard place.

So, there I was, standing in my kitchen, trying to make sense of where some of the boxes that had been stacked in the kitchen had disappeared to when yesterday's mail on the island piqued my curiosity.

Sorting through the small number of envelopes, I opened those I recognized as bills that would need to be paid, and sorted the stuff qualifying as junk, dumping the latter in the recycling bin, which was tucked away by the entry to the garage door.

Hearing Mom in the bathroom reminded me I had breakfast to get ready, so I headed for the fridge to inspect what I had to work with. The rest of the mail could wait.

"Hey, Mom," I said as I opened her bedroom door to see if she would be joining me for breakfast and stopped dead in my tracks, my brows reaching my hairline in surprise at what I saw. "What's going on?" I asked, putting a hand on my hip. "I wanted to check to see if you wanted to join me for breakfast like yesterday.”

“Good morning, sweetheart,” she greeted with a beaming smile. “Actually, I’ve already eaten. Jason’s getting me out of the house today. We figured we’d do some groceries, and maybe stop in at that pub you mentioned, and order a little something to bring home to you for lunch.”

Mother and son grinned at one another. I didn’t miss the conniving little glimmer in her eyes either, which told me today was going to be a good day. One where the Mom of old was creeping through the somber cracks of her reality.

Eyeing my brother, I couldn’t remember hearing or seeing anything out of place that indicated he had come home last night, so instead of going with our current topic of conversation, I answered with a question of my own.

“When did you get home?”

“Around the same time someone left for work this morning,” he answered, his gaze assessing before he turned to our mother. “You ready, Ma?”

“You make sure she’s telling you the truth when you ask her if she’s exhausted,” I told him. “And thanks for looking after the food situation. Don’t forget her mask.”

“No prob, sis,” Jason wrapped one of Mom’s arms around his elbow and ushered them toward her bedroom door, both pausing to kiss my cheek before moving past me. “Enjoy the quiet.”

About two hours later, I was danced out, the floors were shining, and I’d managed to finish what was left of my kitchen organization project.

Upon further investigation, it looked as though Brycen had made himself more than useful after he’d left me and Mom together last night. Spotting the subtlety of things being shifted around, reorganized in such a way that made things easier to be spotted and reached had left me smiling. Some cabinets had been so neatly tidied that I had entire shelves left empty.

The man was magic.

In more ways than one, yet you won't let yourself yield to his sexy ass, my subconscious reminded me for the umpteenth time.

Even though I had no interest in a relationship, I had to admit, Brycen had me thinking. Somehow, with Brycen Matthews, the idea of us being together didn't seem like it would be a hardship in the least.

"Until he decides to leave you for some other hot number," I mumbled, forcing me to remember the disaster that had been my last relationship as a ping came from my phone.

Grabbing it from the counter, I unlocked the screen to discover my brother had sent me a message. Taking the device with me to the living room couch, I sat and answered his latest burning question.

JAY:

So, what's the deal with you and that Brycen guy? BTW, we're now waiting for our lunch order, then Mom and I will be back.

Hurry up, bro, my insides are eating themselves!

And nothing's going on. He's being a good friend, is all.

JAY:

He's got it bad for you. Be careful, sis.

Oh, for fuck's sake!

I'm a grown woman, brother. I know what I'm doing.

JAY:

Not you, it's him I'm worried about.

After what I saw on his face this morning, it's
him getting hurt that concerns me. I know
you're tough as nails, sis.

Before I could text back, Jason's next message popped up.

Order's ready. GTG.

Before I could respond, my phone rang with an unknown number, and because I was preoccupied with thoughts of Brycen, and what my brother had said about the man, I hit the button to connect the call instead of sending it to voicemail.

"'Lo?"

Nothing.

Then deep breathing.

"Hello?" I beckoned, my nerves beginning to stand on end.

Something that sounded like rattling came through, and panic welled within me. Enough that I rushed to my feet and started for the security alarm panel by the front door as I said, "Anyone there?"

Alarm deactivated, the rattling on the other side of the line continued with mixed choking sounds, followed by what sounded like that of wet impact. Horror bloomed to life once more.

"Please say something," I pleaded as I turned the deadbolt to the front door and yanked it open. I wasn't sure who was next on NSI's watch duty roster, and I didn't care. Any of them would be more than competent.

When Cade ran up from down the street, I stopped and felt the tremors take hold of my body. "Please," I whispered. "Who is this?"

The man came to a stop in front of me just as a voice akin to a robot said, "I did it for you, Jana Elway." The line went dead as I simultaneously lost my grip on it—*and* reality.

fourteen

JANA

HOW THE FUCK *does he know my name?* I've never used my last name on calls. It was a cardinal rule of mine. With the slew of wackos out there, that was something I ensured I never did. And there's also the fact I did everything I could to minimize my digital footprint. There was no Facebook, no X, no Instagram for me. I liked my anonymity, something Brycen had been quick to praise once he'd gotten over his shock.

Within moments of having dropped my phone, Cade had grabbed me by my upper arms, ensuring that my legs didn't give out entirely.

"Stay with me, Jana," he ordered, forcing my eyes to meet his. "That's right, girl, keep those eyes on me." I reached for his shirt, the warmth of his person going a long way to steadying me. "That's good. Breathe with me."

He exaggerated every breath, pressing one of his hands to mine for a minute until relief flashed across his face.

"Good," he said as he bent down to pick up my cell. "Now,

let's get you inside. I need to report this incident, but we're going to have a chat before I call it in."

"O-okay," I whispered, not even recognizing my own voice.

CADE

"We got a problem, D," I told my boss as soon as he answered.

"Fu-uck!" Sighing, he proceeded with, "Give it to me, Summers."

At the height of an hour, tops, the whole of NSI had descended and converged in the Elway's living room.

Jana had left the group prior to the final stragglers having arrived, and Jason had taken his mother to her room where she could rest while she ate lunch, and he unpacked the groceries they'd arrived with.

Devolin was the last of the group to show up, having been out of the office when my call had come through.

"Where is she?" the woman demanded, laptop in her bag and at the ready. Her eyes fell on me as she asked, "You got that phone?"

Handing her the device, I warned her. "Go light on her, Huss."

Her tough-as-nails persona disintegrated within a fraction of a second as she nodded in understanding.

"You know I only save the ball-busting for you guys," she stated. "It's par for the course having to work with all you testosterone-filled degenerates every day ending in Y."

Dalton guffawed at his wife's declaration. Just like the boss-man, none of us at NSI would trade having Huss amongst our team for the world. Thank fuck that woman came into our lives when she had.

BRYCEN

"Mind telling me how that fucker got her number?" Jason stormed into the kitchen as soon as I'd headed for it, looking to brew a pot of coffee for the troops, and some glasses, along with a water pitcher I'd spotted last night when I'd done a bit of overhauling in Jana's kitchen. It looked like she'd managed to finish her project sometime after I'd left this morning.

Somehow, our quick tryst I'd put a stop to seemed like it had taken place ages ago instead of mere hours, and all I wanted to do right then was pause and rewind.

"That's what we're working on figuring out," I growled, shutting the refrigerator door a little harder than intended. Depositing the cream and milk on the countertop, I took a few seconds to rein in my fiery temper.

When I turned around to face Jana's brother, his assessing gaze turned to one of almost pity.

"Fuck me," he mumbled, scratching at the scruff on his chin and averting his gaze. "I warned her too late."

"Care to explain that?"

Thankful that Devolin was looking into the cell business, I was able to focus on the security aspect of things with the rest of the guys.

"Got a problem," my boss's wife and cyber partner said as Jana's withdrawn form followed slowly on her heels as they entered the living room from the hall.

As soon as Jana's eyes met mine, I pushed away from my perch against the living room wall, heading straight for her. Grabbing her face gently in both my hands, I aimed her gaze up to mine. "What is it, sweetheart?" She looked worse than when I'd first shown up.

"H-he knows where I live," she said, her voice a hoarse mess and practically undiscernible.

My body stiffened immediately. "Jesus! Fuck!" Stepping away, I turned and let every ounce of frustration overwhelming me out onto the wall next to us, my fist having broken clean through the two layers of drywall as Jana emitted a terrified shriek.

"Christ," Dalton muttered. "Bryce, take a walk, man. You're done."

"Like fuck I am," I growled, and turned to the lady of the house. She wore an uneasy expression, mixed with one of anguish, and it had me instantly feeling like a useless heel—a total prick for terrifying an already scared-shitless woman—*my* woman. "I'm sorry, sweetheart." Without attempting to touch her, I took a step back, then headed for the backyard, shaking my now throbbing hand, and closing only the screen door so I could hear what else might go on.

"Here." Shane's voice knocked me back to the present from the morose thoughts that had infiltrated my head. Turning, I found the man offering me a bag of frozen peas. "Thought you could use it. No one's gonna be able to take a leak without giving everyone else a peepshow from that bathroom until that hole gets patched." The man smirked. "I'll call Theo in," he spoke of a friend and sometimes team member.

"I'll handle it," I told him, gritting my teeth as I applied the makeshift ice pack to my knuckles. "Least I can do for scaring the shit out of her."

"Listen, man," he started, taking a seat on the patio steps beside me. "I know it's hard not to lose it when shit hits the fan with someone we're close to. It's why I warned you off her in the first place."

"I get it, all right?" I huffed my annoyance at his reminder.

"No, you don't, Bryce," he argued. "I warned you off, but that's before I knew this was more than just a passing interest to you." My head turned to look at him so quick, any quicker and I'd have snapped something. "You left so fast, right there, you didn't see the concern on her face. She's worried about you, told Huss as much without realizing I was close enough to overhear."

"What do you suppose I do?"

"Go after her," Jason interrupted, and I turned to look at the newcomer. "Get her out of her head. You're good for her, Matthews. Mom said as much when we were out earlier. Thanks for last night, by the way. I should have been here, but I'm glad she had you." Taking a long breath, his face hardened. "I came out here to let you two know they're talking about moving Jana into a safehouse. I thought you'd want to weigh in on that discussion."

"You'd be fucking right," I grumbled, Shane and I getting to our feet.

Jason gave me a curt nod, meeting my eye. "Good. Now, do me a favor?"

"What's that?"

"Keep her safe." Jason proffered his hand, and I shook it immediately, my eyes glued to his, matching his determination.

"I will."

"Good."

JANA

"And this right here is why I never go on trips," Devolin stated as she helped me pack a few bags, which had rapidly turned into five massive suitcases.

It had been decided, because whoever was after me knew my location, that it would be ultimately safer for Mom, Jason, and me to be relocated. As much as I didn't want to, I knew it was now a necessity. I'd probably have argued more ferociously had it just been me, but it hadn't been that way for months now.

At Dalton's request, Devolin and I were in my bedroom, looking after my things while Jason and Rex were tackling Mom's and my brother's.

"So, tell me about this house Shane's mother owns. Is it

really across the street from where they live?" I asked to keep the conversation going.

"It is. It's also got maxed-out security features, much like this place, but more," she explained, zipping one case closed, then hefting it up to leave it by the bedroom door. "Holy shit-balls, lady! I think you own quadruple the amount of clothes I do."

I couldn't help the giggle that escaped. "I never know how to pack, it doesn't matter whether it's for a few days or a month," I explained.

She nodded, a sad look coming across her face. "I get it. I haven't done much traveling since I was ten, really, unless you count my and Mom's move here from Canada. Being sickly isn't conducive to being a globetrotter, know what I mean?"

I paused long enough to study the other woman. "But you don't look sick," I said. If anything, she looked as if she was glowing. I suppose being with a man who worships the ground you walk on, like Dalton seemed to do, could make anyone look like that. Not for the first time in as little as a few days, I felt envious. Torn.

What would it be like to have a man, not any man, but Brycen, be like that with me?

"That's the thing," she explained, bringing me back to the moment. "Lupus won't always make you sick. Before I met Kip, I'd been in and out of hospitals, mostly in, for nearly two years. A byproduct of childhood cancer treatments leaving me with lupus, and later, aplastic anemia."

Holy shit!

"Yeah, you got that right. Damn well kicked my ass too," she smiled sadly, then shook it off with a grin. A mischievous gleam entered her eyes as she continued telling me her story. "To keep my mind off of my health issues, I got really good at comput-ers." She winked.

A grin to rival hers crept onto my face before I giggled. "We're going to have to get together for a girls' night one of these days, and you're going to have to go into more detail about these computer talents of yours," I announced. Devolin was sweet one minute and had the right degree of sassiness to hold her own with the guys currently crowding my home in the next. I had liked her immediately upon meeting her weeks ago, but this one-one-one time we were having right then had solidified my opinion of her. "So, how'd you and Dalton meet anyway? Brycen told me something about an operation?"

"I suppose." She shrugged her shoulder. "We met unofficially when I stumbled upon a site on the dark web that was making waves about a kidnapped kid." I gulped at the reality. "Officially, we met about a year after that. My jackass uncle called in a favor to see if I could help locate his kidnapped fiancée, who'd disappeared while visiting family in Mexico. I referred him to NSI, but I kept a pulse on things by monitoring online chatter because he's always been into some shady stuff. When I discovered the threat was bigger than what Dalton and his team could ever imagine—and I'm talking cartel big—I convinced my bestie, who's a nurse at the hospital I was admitted to, to let me sneak out so I could warn Dalton."

My eyes rounded at her explanation. "You're shitting me, right?"

She shook her head, no. "I took a cab home, jumped in my car, drove to Kip's house, and when he wasn't there, I went to the next logical place: our friend, Theo's. I should have never left the hospital that day. My nerves got the better of me, and so did my stress levels, and when those get crazy, my lupus sends me into a tailspin."

"Was he there? At Theo's, I mean," I pushed, perched on the edge of the mattress, barely reining in my patience, packing all but momentarily forgotten.

Smiling shyly at her recollection, her eyes sparkled. "Yeah."

"And?" I urged.

"And what? I ended up back in the hospital, the bestie, who turns out to be Dalton's half sister of all things, colluded with my now-dear-husband. To be honest, I think half my heart belonged to him from that first night over the comms," she fessed up. "I've never been one for relationships, and I didn't have the time. I was better at computers and enjoying the small circle of friends I had, because most of everyone in my life had always left. But Dalton never did."

"And I never will, babe," had me jumping out of my skin, my hand clasping at my chest. "Almost ready to go, ladies?" The man walked up to his wife, wrapping an arm around her waist, then kissed the side of her head.

Damn!

"Right?" Devolin smirked as her husband chuckled.

There went my mouth again.

fifteen

JANA

I ACQUIESCED QUITE EASILY, despite the amount of information the NSI crew had thrown at me. Heck, they had totally rearranged my, my brother's, and mother's lives in less than two hours after they'd shown up in my living room.

Plans had changed yet again while Devolin and I had been packing my bags. While Jason and Mom would be moving into the house across from Shane and Emberlyn's, taking Kiki, my Maine coon ball of fur, with them, I was moving to an alternate location—Brycen's decision—based on Cade and Shane's recommendation.

Despite my capitulation to this new and sudden development, the relief I felt at witnessing the support system I clearly had in place this entire time was wearing off. And now, I was beginning to freak the hell out.

It wasn't about the murders.

Well, maybe a little bit. Okay, okay. A lot.

It wasn't about the fact this psycho had managed to figure out my legal name and unearth my phone number, not to mention, he'd also been tracking me via my cell phone.

Yes, maybe that one too.

Nope, it was the fact I was en route to Brycen Matthew's home, with at least a month's worth of personal effects. In addition, said man was one I shouldn't want for myself but did. Furthermore, he seemed obsessed with keeping me safe, more so than the rest of the NSI crew, which was saying a lot, what with the take-charge attitude that had nearly made my house burst at the seams when they'd all converged on my residence earlier. And I'd never had a man look after me like that.

He makes you laugh. He's sweet. And, oh, damn is he hot when he takes charge of a situation you feel you've lost control of!

Yeah, the bulk of my freaking out was largely because I was shacking up with another man, when I'd never planned to do so, after having witnessed all the catastrophic relationships I had in both my childhood and adult life.

Who said you were a couple? It's not really shacking up when you aren't even dating, I reassured myself.

True. It wasn't. Nope. No way. No how.

But what if? the naughty and wanton side of my subconscious whispered, the hussy clearly recognizing Brycen was a breed of man all his own.

"We're here," Brycen's voice broke me from my musings.

Brought back to the present, I looked up to find a beautiful cottage-style, two-story home with a wraparound porch. A light was on in one of the front windows, and the entryway glowed warmly as if it beckoned me forward, welcoming me to my new abode, and urging me to stay a while.

I never noticed Brycen exit his car, but my attention was pulled to him the moment he opened the passenger side door and offered his hand.

"This is your place?" I choked out, my opinion of him having gone up a notch or a hundred. My reticence against exploring the connection between us waned a bit more, as it did every time I discovered something new and entirely unexpected about the man. It endeared him further to me.

I was greeted by a prideful smile. "It is."

I turned back to the property, inspecting it further, and decided immediately that my butt would be enjoying the extra-large egg swing of sorts that was installed in the far front corner of the porch. There was barely any city light pollution where we were, and the sun was setting fast.

It's been forever since I've seen the stars. I can't believe this place exists so close to the city.

"Well, you'll be able to gaze to your heart's content for as long as you're here." I jumped, then whirled around to face the man of the house. With a large warm hand at my hip to steady me, he continued, "Now, let's get you settled in, shall we?"

As we moved toward his front door, I noticed the furry head that peered from the intricately stained-glass pane to the extra-wide, solid wood entryway door.

Brycen inserted the key that would unlock his home, revealing the mysteries within, including the pitiful whining I heard. "Don't mind Bailey. He might be large and in charge, but the only danger you're in is—"

Before I knew it, Bailey had plowed past his owner and pinned me against the railing, his large front paws on my shoulders, a wet tongue laving my face.

"Bailey!" Brycen reprimanded his canine. "Off!"

The dog did as he was told, sitting obediently on his hind quarters, but never looked to his master. Instead, I swore he smiled at me, his long tongue lolling to the right. I couldn't help myself and ruffled the fur atop his head.

"S'okay," I cooed, then crouched down to the dog's level. "You're such a handsome boy, a girl like me could get used to a welcome home like that. I'm just not so sure Kiki would approve."

As I looked up to Brycen, he was grinning at the pair of us.

"Let's get you in here, and I'll get this guy fed and entertained before I make us some dinner. To be honest, I'm not quite sure what I have here." He looked contrite. "It's been a while since I ate in."

My lips tugged up in a smile, and despite where I was, what was going on, who I was with, and how my life had taken a drastic turn toward *Shitsville*, I found myself feeling safe once again. At ease... and at peace for the first time since I'd first woken in my bed, tucked against Brycen today.

BRYCEN

By the time I got back from my backyard fetch session with Bailey, a wonderful smell emanated through the kitchen, toward the patio door entrance.

Sweet Jesus! What the hell is that?

A head of jet-black loosened hair peeked from the top of the island countertop before Jana straightened to her full height.

"Just a casserole," she answered the words I'd thought I'd asked internally. "You had some chicken in the freezer, some breadcrumbs, a pitiful tiny chunk of cheese, some pasta, and a can of cream of mushroom soup. The makings of a kitchen sink casserole. A staple for a single working mother with two young mouths to feed and a small budget."

I groaned, rubbing my belly as I suddenly realized I was famished. "Smells delicious. You didn't have to do this. I said I'd whip something up when I was done. You found everything okay, I take it?"

She nodded. "Go wash up. It should be ready in another five or so. And you," she cooed to my dog, Bailey heading straight for her, "you get this!" She presented him with a small piece of cheese, which he gently took from her fingertips. "Now, go lie down, you good boy."

Without a pause, I watched, amazed that Bailey headed straight for his dog bed in the living room, and the enigma of a woman who intrigued me so much as of late, turned to the kitchen sink and continued to wash dishes.

Turning for the bathroom, I couldn't figure out what was causing the weighted sensation in my chest. It was warm. It was foreign. But I didn't mind it in the least.

Barefoot.

Hair flowing freely.

Curvy hips swayed from side to side at the sink to whatever song she was beautifully humming to herself.

Unguarded and at ease. Jana's subtle presence in my home, seeing her like this had my cock standing at attention.

I rubbed at the scruff on my chin, all the while continuing to study her. What was it about this woman?

"Oh!" She clasped a hand to her chest, a washcloth haphazardly held in her other. "I thought you were watching the news."

Feeling much like getting caught with my hand in the cookie jar, I smirked, sheepishly shrugging the shoulder opposite the one I was using to lean against the front of the refrigerator.

"Wanted to make sure you didn't need any help." Sure. Let's call it that, even though Brycen Jr. down there wanted to make sure of other things. Dark, hot, and wet things. Things that weren't exactly appropriate with my current duties entailing this woman's safety, no matter her mother's and brother's joint blessings *to go for it.*

"Brycen?"

Next thing I knew, Jana was standing toe to toe with me. I was so deep in my wanton thoughts I hadn't noticed she'd moved.

"Huh?"

"Did you hear me?"

Licking my lips, I cleared my throat and mumbled, "No... sorry."

Fucker, take your eyes off her mouth! But the moment I aimed my gaze to hers, I realized I'd made a horrible mistake.

sixteen

JANA

OH, *God!*

I really didn't know what to do with the way Brycen was looking at me.

This can't be happening.

One minute, we were behaving like normal adults—friends even—and in the next, I had this beautiful man before me, looking as hungry as a wolf, appearing as though he wanted to gobble me up like I was a rabbit.

I'm sure women would swoon over less than that desire-filled gaze of his.

But swoon I couldn't.

I swore I wouldn't give in to my baser instincts—at least not yet. We'd both agreed just that morning. And my life was in shambles.

Despite my suddenly swollen tongue, parched mouth, and dry lips, I managed, "Hand." Brycen's eyes flared impossibly hotter, so I cleared my scratchy throat and added, "I'm tired. Let me doctor your hand, and then I'm going to head to bed. You'll have to ice it again when I'm done though."

With a shake of his head and a step back, Brycen emitted an "Oh...uh..." swallowed, and proceeded with, "O-okay."

"Where's that first aid kit you mentioned on the car ride here?"

"Kitchen sink," he responded, taking a seat at the kitchen table, a look of confusion—or was it rejection—strewn across his beautiful face.

What a long night.

How Brycen hadn't called me on my evasiveness by doctoring his hand, then escaping for his spare bedroom at a little past eight in the evening, I'll never know. Thankfully, I had my own bathroom and a television, which enhanced my seclusion.

Nearly three hours later, after having bathed in some fancy bubble bath, coupled with candlelight, and some music from one of my trusty Spotify playlists, I was just starting to doze, when light enshrined my entire bedroom, followed by the loudest bang point-five seconds later.

A surprised shriek snuck out and delight at the electricity in the air filled me.

I loved thunderstorms. Always had, and probably always would. But it also meant I wouldn't be sleeping until it let up. Storms typically energized me to the point I was obsessed with watching Mother Nature's light show. It was the rain that followed that generally relaxed and lulled me into a fitful slumber afterward.

In nothing but a thin tank top and some lounge shorts, I added thick wool socks to keep my feet warm, then grabbed the throw from the foot of my bed. Wrapping the soft material around my shoulders, I tiptoed out of my room and headed for the front door. I knew exactly where I'd most likely get the best show, therefore, I headed for that egg-shaped swing thing on Brycen's porch.

. . .

BRYCEN

Jana hadn't spotted me as she snuck out the front door. If I'd hazard a guess, I'd say she had taken the opportunity—being the reasonable adult—and had made her escape earlier to avoid the attraction that undoubtedly had grown exponentially between us over the last few days. The spooked look in her eyes had given her away, and neither of us were in the right head-space to test the proverbial waters.

So, here I was, in the present, feeling like a creeper for sitting in the dark, watching the woman of my most recent fantasies trying in vain to cover her shapely thighs and legs with a small throw as she cozied herself up in my porch swing.

The peaceful look on her face following each lightning flash had me entranced.

She loved thunderstorms.

So did I, in fact. And Bailey...not so much. The big lug was currently cowering in the back of my walk-in closet after having knocked everything out of his way so he could be as deep as could be in his self-made den of safety.

Standing by one of the living room's windowed sliders, the sight of the woman shivering at the abrupt gust of wind made my mind up for me.

Heading to the kitchen, I set the kettle to boiling and grabbed the two large mugs from beside the coffee maker which I'd left before deciding to call it a night shortly before Jana had come out of her room. Reaching for the pantry, I grabbed a couple tea bags and dropped one in each mug before filling both with the ready boiled water.

"Ah, the interloper finally joins," she said softly, her eyes remaining on the sky as soon as I slid the door open. "I was wondering when you'd stop creeping and come out."

"I brought something to warm you up," I said, presenting

her with a mug of tea, which she accepted readily, not pushing for me to acknowledge her earlier statement. "It's chamomile."

She studied me for a split second and her eyes filled with humor. "You drink chamomile?" She brought the cup up to her lips, savoring the smell of the liquid before taking a small sip to test its temperature and taste.

"My sisters like to make sure I have all the fixings," I explained. "They claim that it's half the battle to be able to bring a woman over and have her want to stay."

Jana grinned.

"I never had the heart to tell them to stop, and some of the shit they bring over is actually pretty good." I shrugged.

"And the woman part?" she inquired.

"No woman has set foot in this house that I haven't been related to." My eyes met and held hers in all seriousness. "Until you."

Jana froze at my statement.

To break the awkwardness of my truth, I pulled the large lounging chair closer to the swing and made myself comfortable. Jana's long legs stretched out, her feet meeting the edge of my chair's cushion for swinging leverage. My hands itched to lean forward and run them over her smooth skin. Instead, I clasped both around my large mug and forced myself to remain a gentleman—a friend. It's what the poor woman needed more than anything right then anyhow. Anything else would fall into place, eventually, if Lady Fate would allow it.

"Couldn't sleep?" I asked at the same time she said, "Sorry about earlier."

"Don't be."

"I just didn't—" She broke her own progress, sighed, then looked to the sky as if it would provide her with the right words. Instead, she led with, "To be honest, I was just fading into sleep when the storm started. I can never sleep during these things because I prefer to watch them."

Let it slide, Bryce. If she wasn't ready to bring up the proverbial elephant in the room about our undoubtable attraction, then I wasn't going to force anything.

"I kind of gathered that when I saw you walk by me in the dark and come out here," I smirked.

"There's just something about watching Mother Nature come alive," she explained.

I nodded, then added, "I agree." Her eyes were still aimed skyward.

"What about you?" she questioned, meeting my gaze. "What were you doing sitting in the dark?"

I wasn't really going to tell her about my internal debate on if I should go to her and apologize about earlier; at least, not yet.

"Couldn't seem to fall asleep," I said instead. "Probably because, under normal circumstances, I'm still working at this time."

Jana looked alarmed and a wee bit guilty. "Am I preventing you from doing your job by being here?"

"If anything, Dalton would probably say you're a good influence, in the sense you got me out of the office and kept me away from my dungeon, which led to an early bedtime." I couldn't help the self-deprecating smile. "Like I've mentioned before, I'm a workaholic."

"Dungeon?" Jana's eyes were wide, her soft pouty lips pursed.

"It's what I call my home office. It's in the basement because it's so large, and the women in my life think it's better suited for a man cave than in all the *good number of bedrooms* I'm meant to fill," I told her.

That tinkling giggle of hers graced my ears, then was chased by a flash of light in the distance, and another loud rumble of thunder.

"How many sisters?"

"Three. I'm the youngest." The look of horror on her face

had me laughing out loud. "Yes, it was as horrific as you're imagining it in that pretty little head of yours."

She shook her head. "Oh, you don't want to know what's going through my head right now."

Her suggestive and teasing tone caused a certain part of my anatomy to take notice, and I leaned forward, not only to hide its appearance, but also because she had me enthralled in what her thoughts about my upbringing would entail.

"Please, nothing could top the times they put in barrettes and tried to braid my hair. I was like their own personal baby doll for most of my early years," I said. "I've woken up many times with painted toenails, lipstick. Hell, Cora even managed to convince me to try her eyelash curler when I was eight."

Jana's laugh pierced the night, and I was smitten, reveling in the fluttering sensation in my chest.

"You're close," she stated rather than asked.

I nodded. "We are. All three are married now, and I'm an uncle five times over, and a sixth on the way. I don't see everyone as much as I'd like to, but at least twice a month or so, I'll join Dad for a day of fishing, and we have family dinners every Sunday that, I'll admit, I miss more often than anyone and myself would like."

Jana's expression fell from dreamlike to sad. "That sounds beautiful...and amazing." I simply nodded. "And I take it your parents are still together?"

My grin only widened. "They are. I swear, I've never seen any two people so in love as they are, except for maybe D and Huss—that's Dalton and Devolin. Shane and Emberlyn, as well as Cade and his new woman, Aspen, are close seconds. Their love is one for the ages. My parents have been together since Mom was seventeen and Dad was nineteen. They've been married for forty-four years. Forty-five in a few months."

"Wow!"

"I know. I'd like to have something like them some day," I

confessed. Jana didn't say anything, so I prompted her. "How 'bout you?"

"Everyone I know hasn't had much luck with marriage and relationships," she began, "yours truly included. I used to think everyone has a soulmate, but once I became an adult, the sparkle of the idea faded away. Once bitten, twice shy, you know?"

I did. "Yeah."

"It's not that I've given up on the idea of love and a happy ending for myself; it's just I don't think it's in the cards for me."

"So, you've sworn off men?"

"Not really. It's just I don't feel I need a man to help me through life."

"Feminist?" I teased, making her laugh lightly.

"All for women taking a stand and pursuing their life goals and being successful. If that's the level of feminism you're asking about, then I suppose, yeah."

"So, you're egalitarian? You believe that women should be able to do whatever a man can, equal pay, et cetera?"

"You got it." She pointed a finger at me while still cradling her mug in both hands.

"What about your family?" Jana cringed. "Sore point? I'm sorry, you don't have to answer that."

"No, it's okay. Let's just say there's nothing to write home about. Mom and my father split when I was two. I've never seen the man again, but if you're asking if Jason, my mother, and I are close, you already know we are. We try to have time where all three of us are together, but with Jason's and my schedules, since they've moved in with me, it's been tough. And now, with Mom's health declining further, and..."

seventeen

JANA

"AND NOW, with Mom's health declining further, and…"

My eyes fought a losing battle with the onslaught of tears. Everything that had been going on became simply too much for me to deal with, even though I'd thought I'd be good for a bit after last night's purge.

I hiccupped, attempted to take a sip from my tea, but the bubble of emotion in my throat prevented me from doing so. Setting down the cup on the side table nearby, I braced for what was to come.

Looking at Brycen was a complete and utter mistake.

The empathy in his expression broke the dam.

And my heart shattered.

"Shit!" I heard the man curse, and next thing I knew, he was at my feet, draping his arms across my lap, holding one of my hands as the other served at holding the throw around my shoulders, clutching it as if it were a lifeline, lest I unravel entirely should I release its hold.

Memories, old and recent, poured to the forefront of my mind.

My mother would never meet her grandchildren if Jason or myself were to have any, unless either one of us ended up with child, like yesterday. There would be no one to walk us down the aisle at either of our weddings. There would be no more family dinners, reunions with aunts and uncles, where Mom would be at the center of the crazy traditions and other such shenanigans.

Then anger replaced my sadness.

"All that fucking radiation. The chemo. A double mastectomy. And for what?" I screamed over the thunder ahead.

A large, warm hand began rubbing my bare thigh, as soothing words made their way to my ears.

"I'm so sorry, sweetheart. I can't even begin to imagine, or to know what you're feeling right now. I—"

"It's not fair!"

"It's not."

"She hasn't really lived her life."

"No, she hasn't."

"She never found someone else to love."

"No, but she loves you and Jason so much. Anyone with eyes can see it, sweetheart."

"She's always been there for us."

"It's what moms do, babe."

The man had me vexed. "Would you fucking stop simply agreeing with me?"

His eyes remained soft with an undertone of confusion. "Sorry?"

"You're agreeing with everything I'm saying. Why can't you —" *be angry with me?*

Because anger was easier to deal with than the despair I was feeling. Then again, my tears weren't letting off, despite the rage that burbled inside me.

"Sweetheart?"

I tore my gaze from his, setting it instead on the night sky. "What am I going to do?"

"Come 'ere," he said, and next thing I knew, strong hands pulled at my ass—even though I was pretty sure he had aimed to grasp my waist—and I dropped from the egg chair onto his lap, where strong arms wrapped themselves around me, trapping me against his chest, my head on his shoulder, and arms tucked between us. "You can be sad. You can be angry. Hit something. Hit me. Cry. Scream. Rant. Vent. I don't care what you do, because I think you need to feel all of this right now. Let it out, sweetheart. I got you."

His words broke me down. Had anyone else said the same, they would have incited my fury. Like Jason as an example.

But Brycen isn't your brother.

Oh, God no! No, he wasn't. Far from that.

Taking in the strong muscular arms surrounding me, the warmth of his chest against my arms, the strength of his legs under my ass, I collapsed against him and simply let go.

BRYCEN

It could have been hours, seconds...probably closer to a few minutes later, I heard Jana whisper, "I still need her."

It broke my heart, but instead of saying anything, I simply tightened my grasp on the woman. She relaxed farther into my hold, flattening the palms of her hands against my chest while sobbing softly.

She felt warm. *Right*, like she had every time before.

Fuck me! This was a new level of hell for me.

Being the little brother in a family of four kids had me at an advantage with the fairer sex and the multitude of exploding emotions that came with them. It didn't scare me like most men would be put off by them. If I may say so myself, I thought I was pretty good at the consoling thing.

Until tonight.

When Jana asked me why I was so agreeable, I had a sense she was asking me why I wasn't angry with her instead.

She's not your sisters.

Nope. No, she wasn't. She'd become so much more than that in the short time I'd gotten to know her. Beyond her looks, she had a fiery personality I couldn't help but adore. Heck, as I sat here holding her on my lap, I wondered how she'd look furious. I knew her laugh, her smiles, the way she became almost despondent when trouble came her way. I now knew how she tried to hide her sadness behind frustration and bravery. And I wanted more. I needed to know all the nuances in between those emotions, so I could read her like a book. More importantly, I wanted Jana to know me, and not just flirty Brycen Matthews, computer savant and hacker extraordinaire. *Me.*

"Your legs are going to go dead," Jana finally mumbled, her subtle body shudders having dissipated.

"Not a chance," I said and kissed her hair, squeezing her to me.

"Let me—"

"You're fine right where you are, sweetheart," I stated.

With a slight pressure to my chest, Jana pulled back to look at me. "Thanks."

I gave her a sad smile. "Anytime."

She looked confused. "Why aren't you looking more freaked out?"

"Sisters, remember?"

Her lips crept upward ever so slightly at their edges. "Right."

Our eyes held, and silence was filled with the sounds of thunder in the distance. The storm was ebbing.

When her gaze traveled to my lips, I subconsciously licked them, causing her bright eyes to darken to the most intense emerald green.

Cupping the side of her face, my other hand remained on the middle of her back to support her, I leaned in and kissed her forehead. "Better?" I asked as I pulled away to find her face looking peaceful, her once opened eyes now closed as if savoring the moment.

"Mmm." When her eyes opened once more, they were clear of the darkness, trouble, and desire they once held. "Yes. Thank you."

"We should go to bed." My voice came out sounding hoarse. "It's getting late."

"We should," she agreed, then proceeded to get up, offering me her hand, which I took.

In mere minutes, we were once again inside my home, the doors locked tight, and I had escorted Jana to her bedroom door before heading for my own.

"Brycen?"

"Yeah?" I turned to find that Jana, still enshrouded in that throw she'd been cuddling with, hadn't opened her door.

She quickly came my way, placed a single hand to my chest, leaned up on her tiptoes and placed her lips to my cheek. "Thank you."

Words evading me, I simply nodded my welcome.

"Goodnight." As quickly as she'd kissed me, she disappeared behind the spare bedroom door.

eighteen

JANA

WHEN MY ALARM WENT OFF, I simply wanted to bash the stupid thing until it lay on the floor in a heap of plastic and electronic components. My face felt puffy, eyes gritty as if a sandstorm had forced the tiny grains under my eyelids while I slept. That and my churning stomach served to prove that although I'd slept, I'd received little rest last night.

Dragging my sorry ass out of bed, ready to apologize for using Brycen as a crying cushion, I decided putting on any airs would be useless. One look in the bathroom vanity mirror proved no amount of concealer would cover the dark bags under my eyes. It might tone down the redness in my face, especially the tip of my nose, but what was the use?

Grabbing the throw I'd used last night, I covered up and sauntered toward the kitchen, the wonderful aroma of melted butter, eggs, bacon...and coffee adding a little urgency to my stride.

My steps halted when I spotted Brycen sitting at the kitchenette table, a pinched look to his face as he flexed his hand, a discarded ice pack sitting next to a steaming cup of coffee, and Bailey lay at his feet.

I caused that. And my heart wanted to do anything to take his pain away—to take the inconvenience of having me to worry about out of this man's daily equation.

Bailey whined, lifting his head to greet me. The dog's golden eyes seemed to beg that I do something, *anything*, to help his master.

Before I knew it, I was crouched down in front of Brycen, taking his injured hand in mine to examine it. A few scrapes, one nasty gash that looked angry red, and some bruising marred his skin. "Did you ice it last night?" I demanded.

"Uhm," was all that came out, but the guilty look in his eyes told me all I had to know.

"Right," I huffed, propping his hand on the table's edge, and went to fetch the first aid kit we'd used last night.

Walking by the stove, I noticed he'd completed his cooking duties, everything must have been in the oven, keeping warm for when I woke up as I spotted the telltale light letting me know the device was working its magic.

Good. It gave me time to doctor the man up. Stupid fool! *Sweet fool*, my subconscious amended.

Taking to my knees with the kit in hand, I spread the bag open, revealing everything I'd need, and more.

"What'd I do?" he asked. My brows furrowed in askance. "You called me a fool. What'd I do?"

"I noticed you didn't keep the bandage on," I stated. "It's my fault you're hurt, and if this gash gets infected, then that'll be my fault too," I growled, then shoved the edge of an alcohol swab packet in my mouth, tearing it with a single hand. "This is gonna sting," I warned.

"How's it your fault?"

"Since I can't seem to hold it together, you flew off the handle." I paused long enough to meet his gaze. "See? My fault."

"The hell it is," he growled.

Next thing I knew, he'd hefted me from under my arms, and up so I straddled his lap, sitting reverse on the chair, our chests colliding.

"Brycen, no!" I scolded him, pushing back, but his arms were firmly wrapped around me, thwarting my escape. "Let me clean your hand."

"I can clean my own damn hand," he grouched. "Let's get one thing straight here." Keeping a single hand at my back to prevent my retreat, his injured hand reached for my chin and held it firmly between his fingers so I couldn't look away.

"I swore I'd protect you, and I haven't been doing a great job of it, Jana."

"But—"

"I should have checked your fucking phone after he'd had that package delivered to your office," he explained. "Should have covered all the bases, and that meant looking for any kind of tracker."

"But, Bryce—"

"When you came out of that room..." His expression was one of regret—guilt. "Fuck, baby." He shook his head on a disgusted huff. "I was ready to rage on someone, *something*."

"That's not your fault. Even Devolin blamed herself for not thinking of it," I told him. "She told me as much when she found it. Honestly, I don't think anyone would have been the wiser had he not called."

His jaw grew tight, tension surrounded his mouth. "Should have known better," he argued. "It's the fact you have an almost inexistent cyber footprint that distracted me from thinking about your phone."

Acknowledging this was a great opportunity to give him some comfort in return for all he'd done for me thus far, I leaned in, touching my forehead to his, offering a small smile.

"It's over now. Dev figured it out, we have a plan in place, and everyone's safe, Brycen," I whispered, the man having closed his eyes to hear me out. "Now, can I please clean and bandage your hand? I'd like to get to that breakfast you so nicely cooked for us."

Those dark chocolaty pools of his opened and captured my gaze. "My hand can wait a minute," he whispered, his fingers shifting so his hand could hold the side of my neck. "I just have to—"

"Bryce—" I tried to be the rational one.

But he cut me off with his lips.

BRYCEN

It wasn't a heated kiss per se, more one that conveyed my gratitude for her worry about my stupidity that led to my sore hand. It was a kiss that reassured me she was indeed here, in my home, my sanctuary. That she trusted me, and the guys at NSI, to do our thing and catch the sicko who was after her. It also went a long way, with how she responded, that this attraction between us wasn't fading anytime soon.

Pulling away, Jana's hand came up, touching my lips with her fingers, and I couldn't help but kiss them.

With a shy smile, she made to get to her feet, and I allowed it, reminding myself that slow and steady might be just what it took me to win this proverbial race.

I'd left Jana to her devices, with Bailey looking after her in my large backyard as they chased each other around the yard and played fetch. With the breakfast dishes done and stowed away at Jana's insistence that she clean after I'd cooked, I'd ensured that she was settled before retreating to my basement office.

Checking in with Devolin, she'd managed to make a dent into things, leaving me with little to do, aside from looking after a new phone and number be issued for my current roommate. Turns out, the unsub—or unknown subject—we were chasing was knowledgeable about technology, just not as well-versed as we were.

The fucker had hacked into Jason's computer with the aid of a worm. Looked like Jana's brother wasn't as concerned about leaving digital crumbs everywhere he went online. Where his sister had little to no internet presence, the same couldn't be said about her brother. I'd have to have a talk with him about beefing up his web security, especially what with the sites he was quite prolific in visiting. Between those habits along with another, where he'd opened some unsolicited emails, it had been more than enough for our man to infiltrate Jana's phone.

Turned out Jana had opened a video attachment in a text her brother had sent her. The rest was history.

"So, this is where you've been hiding." She had me jumping in my seat, swiveling my desk chair around to face my interloper. "Gotta say...wow!" The look on Jana's face told me she was more than impressed as she stepped inside the large room and took everything in. "That's quite the setup you've got here. And I thought having four monitors at work was a challenge in adjustment to your typical nine-to-five desk jockey job."

I grinned and shrugged. "Same kind of setup I have at the office, as a matter of fact, except slightly on a smaller scale. Devolin has her own corner in our techno hub too. Everything I do there I can do here, though," I explained.

Jana's eyes froze on one of the TV monitors up on my wall, nearest to me. "You were watching?" she asked, not so much as accused. When her eyes met mine, they held nothing but warmth and acceptance.

"This whole place is wired, inside *and* out," I said. "I'm sorry, I should have said something earlier, but—"

Her smile had some of my remaining apprehension faltering. "No, it's okay," she sighed and shrugged. "Kind of makes me feel safe if you're not close by."

To break the silence that had momentarily fallen between us, I asked, "So, what's up?"

"I was gonna ask if you'd planned to spend your entire Saturday in this mecca of yours and starve, or if you wanted to join me for an early dinner and a movie or a dozen."

"Mecca, huh?" I got to my feet, and stretched, not missing the dip of her interested gaze to my midsection, where my shirt bisected away from the top of my jeans while my arms were above my head.

"Uhm." Her eyes trailed from my stomach, down to my crotch. In seconds, most likely once she'd realized what she'd done and shaken herself of whatever thoughts were running through that pretty head of hers, her eyes skyrocketed to meet mine. A light blush suffused her face as she bit her bottom lip, then said, "Uh, yeah."

Caught in her ogling, I grinned, studying her long enough as I ran a hand over the scruff on my chin. She squirmed subtly due to my direct attention. "I could do food...and a movie, but that depends on what you have in mind to watch."

Her eyes narrowed on me. "No chick flicks, if that's what you thought."

On a short laugh, I held my hands up in a peacekeeping gesture and smirked. "Just saying I'd be okay with it if it was really what you wanted to watch, but I'm more of a psychological thriller kind of guy."

"Thought I'd figured you for some sort of military fanatic about SEALs, Green Berets, or some kind of World War movie buff." Her smile matched mine as she self-assuredly crossed her arms over her chest. "How do you feel about horror?" The look I gave her must have belied my disbelief, because her smile turned into a full-out grin as she shrugged. "Figured, with October around the corner, might as well take this downtime of mine and indulge in some Wes Craven, Stephen King, and maybe a few Rob Zombie flicks. Might get me out of my head today since reading isn't helping me any."

"Found the AMC or Shudder channels on my Prime account, have you?" I chuckled.

That subtle blush from earlier pinkened her cheeks once more. "Might have." Clearing her throat, she proceeded. "I ordered some Chinese since it's slim pickings in your kitchen. There's probably going to be enough to last us a week because I wasn't sure what you liked, so I ordered a variety, and paid cash in case you were worried about someone monitoring my cards."

Taking a step toward her so we stood toe to toe, my hand seemed to have a mind of its own as it cupped her cheek and tilted her face so I could really look at her. As beautiful as she was, I could make out the lines of stress and strain marring her features, and the bags beneath her eyes that proved she'd gotten little if any sleep last night, much like I hadn't, after the storm had passed. Despite those temporary flaws, she was still the most beautiful creature in my book—and a smart one— color me impressed that she'd taken it upon herself to minimize being tracked by whomever we were chasing.

"I'll make sure NSI reimburses you for that, and I'll place an order for groceries before the end of the day," I promised, sealing my words with a quick peck to her lips. When I pulled away, shocked at my forwardness, I was struck by the humored smile slowly making itself known on Jana's mouth. Instead of overanalyzing things, I opted to act aloof, sidestepping her, then led the way back upstairs. When she didn't follow imme- diately, I added a, "Coming?" never pausing to wait. When the telltale sound of scurrying footsteps trying to catch up with me came, the wide grin that spread on my face held encourage- ment. I wasn't the only one who felt off-kilter every time we were in close proximity.

nineteen

Jana

MICHAEL HAD JUST BEEN DEFEATED for the umpteenth time, by his seven-year-old niece and her entourage, when I'd taken my final bite of General Tso chicken, while Brycen had left his polished off plate on the coffee table a few minutes ago.

As the end credits rolled on *Halloween IV*, I washed down my final bite of food with a sip of iced water, feeling Brycen's eyes on the side of my face.

Fixating on the man, I wondered if I had food on my face, or something more embarrassing was up with my appearance. "What?" I set my plate to the side and proceeded to give my mouth, chin, and cheek another cursory wipe with my napkin.

Brycen simply shook his head, sporting a grin on his mug, his gaze intent on me, a gleam of humor and curiosity in his eyes, as though he was trying to figure something out.

"Brycen," I urged him, feeling even more self-conscious the longer he remained mum. "What is it?"

He scrubbed at his scruffy chin, the memory of how that scruff had felt so briefly on my face with that peck he'd given me in his office. The thought had my girlie bits warming, my mind wondering how it would feel on other places other than over my chin, my cheeks...

"Just trying to figure you out," he stated, his index reaching out to flick my nose before he got up from the couch we'd been sharing, and grabbed both our plates, proceeding toward the kitchen.

"What?" I looked at his retreating back quizzically, then got up with his empty drinking glass and mine, following him.

"She's into slasher flicks, reads risqué romance novels, limits her electronic footprint, turns my dog into a puddle of goo with just a few words, loves her family fiercely, is dedicated to her job in helping random strangers, makes sure I'm fed, and she's hot as fuck," he rambled in a mumbled fashion as he stacked our soiled dishes in the dishwasher after having rinsed them, his back still to me. Looking at the ceiling, he sighed heavily before shaking his head, then bending to stuff the last utensil in the washer. "I'm fucking screwed."

Setting our glasses down on the counter next to where he stood, Brycen startled when I wrapped my arms around him from behind. His warm hand covered both of mine. "I'm trying really hard here to find something about you that will completely turn me off, and thus throw us back onto the platonic side of things, Jana, but for the love of Christ, I can't," he confessed, then turned in my arms as soon as I released the hold I had on him so he could face me.

Uh oh.

"Tell me not to, and I won't," he whispered, an arm surrounding me, bringing my front flush with his, his face hovering mere inches from mine, eyes searching.

I can't.

In an instant, his irises turned to molten chocolate, then his lips were on mine, making my world tilt on its axis, propelling me headfirst into Brycen Matthews and all he was willing to offer.

. . .

BRYCEN

Perfection.

Jana gave as much as she took. When my lips met hers this time, it was as if something finally clicked between us.

The feel of her softness against my hard, the willingness to not fight whatever this attraction between us that brewed to a boiling point was overwhelming.

I'm not even sure she knew she'd said those two words aloud: *I can't.* The moment they'd escaped that irresistible mouth of hers, it cemented the fact she was open to exploring things on a more intimate level. Whatever fight and reservation that was left in her had simply vanished the moment I'd run my mouth about what I thought of her. I hadn't figured she'd follow me to the kitchen, so I'd rambled a slew of things I never meant for her ears to hear until I was ready to fully open up.

Steering us backward so my ass hit the counter's edge, Jana's hands feathered through the short, cropped hair at the back of my head, her blunt nails digging in, setting my blood on fire.

The moment my hands cupped her ass, gaining a sweet palmful of tush, a throaty moan escaped her, inciting her to rub her chest against mine as if she were a cat in heat.

On a groan of my own, I grabbed her by the ass, she hopped up, and wrapped her legs around me as I reversed our position. Setting her down on the counter, it gained me a hiss once her thighs made contact with the cool granite, thanks to those lounge shorts she was wearing.

Her legs pulled me in, and I could feel her needful heat through our layers of clothes.

"Sweetheart," I mumbled through kisses, slowing things down slightly, kissing the side of her mouth, making my way to her cheek, lower still to the delicate curve where her neck met her shoulder. "Fuck," I growled, "I could kiss you forever."

I pulled away to take in her kiss-swollen mouth, and the scruff burn on her face.

"You kiss like a fucking dream," she moaned and tried to pull me back to her, and I went willingly, offering her a soft peck. "I think I could come with just your kisses alone." Her hands lightly slid from my shoulders down the front of my shirt, until she got to its hem, where she surreptitiously began to lift it up my torso as she lined my jaw with kisses.

Assisting her with its removal, chucking the cotton T-shirt to the side, Jana's face pulled back enough for her eyes to feast on my bared skin, her hands perusing the naked flesh of my chest.

"You're a work of finely honed art, Brycen Matthews," she marveled before depositing a soft kiss over my left pectoral.

"And you're about to take this to a level I never imagined us going tonight," I groaned when her tongue came out to flick my nipple.

Pulling back again, her eyes met mine, fire alight in her gaze. "I was sitting there"—she delivered a sweet kiss to the side of my mouth before continuing—"thinking I had food on my face, or that a bee's nest had formed in my hair after having spent the afternoon lazing on your couch." She kissed the other side. "And then you said those things..." Her voice trailed off, and she swallowed hard.

Cupping her face in my hands, I watched as she struggled with finding the right words, reassuring her with a soft kiss of my own, directly to her mouth.

"You see me," she whispered, closing her eyes, "and it terrifies the fuck out of me."

"And why is that?" I asked right as I tilted her head and deposited a kiss to her forehead. I knew her reasoning went beyond her mother's failed relationship with her father, or any of her unworthy exes.

Finally, gracing me with those emerald orbs of hers, filled with emotion and so much lust I could burst in my pants from looking into them too long, she confessed. "Because you have staying power."

JANA

"Explain," Brycen urged. As I tried to evade his eyes, his hands held fast, gently keeping my face aimed toward his eyes, trapping me in his sincere and caring, not to mention, smoldering gaze.

"You've stuck around when you could have pawned me off to one of your coworkers. I've done nothing but been a train wreck since we met, crying and sniveling all over you," I bared my shame. "I've been cold more than warm toward you, so despite our common interests in something as mundane as slasher flicks, almond chicken guy ding, and General Tso chicken, or pizza and beer, I was failing to see what you see in me."

When he dropped his hands from the sides of my face in order to cover my hands over his chest, I retreated partially, averting my face.

"When you stated all of those things about me, you saw more of me than I thought I'd allowed you to see."

"Look at me," he gentled. When I didn't, his tone, although sweet, carried a hint of command to it. "Baby, look at me." So, I did, and when our eyes connected, I wanted to cut and run about as much as I wanted to hold on to him and never let go. "I'm not one of your good-for-nothing exes, who ditches you at the first sign of trouble, Jana. I have staying power because, from the moment we had our first conversation, I was drawn in. I had to know you. And the more of you I get to know, woman..." He paused to shake his head, his features transforming into a baffled expression. "You've had me enthralled in every nuance of you." He buffed my lips with his. "Now, this evening has gotten heavier than I could have imagined, and although unplanned, I can't say I regret all of this coming out."

"You don't?"

He shook his head. "Not for a hot minute, babe. It just means that I'm in here." He gingerly tapped the side of my temple, smiling. "And in here." He tapped my breastbone next. "And heaven forbid lightning strikes me down for sounding crass, but someday soon...not today, mind you, I might just get in here." He slid his hand so his palm broke the connection between our crotches, palming the raging heat at the apex of my thighs with a wicked grin.

Just as soon as he touched me intimately, his digits disappeared, and his face grew serious with intent. "For right now, as much as I'll most likely be spending a sleepless night kicking myself for what I'm about to say, I think it might be best if I were to put my shirt on, take you back to the couch, and protect you from the death and turmoil that Michael Myers will be bringing forth in the rest of our *Halloween* franchise marathon." He delivered a chaste but no-less-potent kiss to my lips, pulling away to smile slyly. "What do you say?"

Feeling slightly playful, despite our emotionally turbulent conversation and assorted confessions, I returned his smile, albeit with a flirty one of my own. "I say, leave the shirt, I'll match you in removing this sweater, and we can do as you want, cocooned in a blanket." Ensuring I'd made my request clear, I pulled my right hand from his chest, wrapped it behind his neck, then pulled him to me for an all-too-short kiss, ending it with a slight nibble to his bottom lip. "What do *you* say?"

Grinning, his eyes sparkling with mirth, he shook his head in disbelief. "I say you've got a deal, you little vixen." Kissing my forehead, he pulled away, helping me hop off the counter before releasing me altogether to finish putting our glasses in the dishwasher. Flipping its door shut with his foot, he headed for the fridge. "Wine? Beer? Something weaker? Stronger?"

"Beer is good," I said, knowing it was his preferred social drink of choice. "I'll go cue up number five," I added, turning to exit the kitchen, proceeding to remove the sweater I was wearing, knowing all too well that his eyes were on me when my threadbare tank top made its appearance—sans bra.

twenty

BRYCEN

BY THE TIME the credits rolled to the final *Halloween* movie, I was blissed out, yet in absolute hell at the same time.

Jana had fallen asleep about halfway through, the events of the last few weeks, and last night's lack of sleep having caught up to her.

Turning the TV off, then setting the remote on the end table at my side, I took a moment to study the woman who was wrapped up in my couch throw, her head on my lap, my fingers tangled in her soft hair where they'd stayed as I'd periodically massaged her scalp, intermittently tugging at the strands on and off while we vegged together.

The wit she'd displayed about the stupidity of the movie characters in their clear aversion to run like their asses were on fire, or the less than stellar horrified bloodcurdling screams, citing she could teach them a thing or two, had us laughing.

Honestly, it had been the most innocent and relaxed fun I'd had in far too long. Having Jana in my home, hanging out, despite the undeniable attraction we shared, felt as if she'd always been part of my life, even though we'd only met three weeks ago.

I hadn't lied to Jana last night. Aside from my female relatives, and coworkers' women, I'd never brought anyone I'd dated home—let alone had anyone in my bed. I'd never wanted to, until now.

Caught in my thoughts of what this latest revelation meant, I felt Jana stir in her sleep, her hand making its way to meet the one that was still tangled in her hair, to squeeze it.

"Is the movie over already?" she whispered in a sleep-roughened voice, her slumberous gaze meeting mine.

"Just a few minutes ago," I told her, running my fingertips against her scalp again. "We should get you to bed." I swear she purred at the subtle pressure of my digits.

"I love it when you do that," she whispered with her eyes closed, a blissed-out expression on her face. "But if you keep doing that, I'll pass out again."

Straightening herself to a seated position, she rubbed at her eyes, a sleep-drunk smile tugging at the edges of her lips as she twisted around so her knee pressed against my thigh, her hand coming to settle on it.

"Thanks for today." Her eyes met mine.

"Don't mention it," I mumbled. "I think I needed this about as much as you did."

"Mmm." Her eyes dropped to my chest before meeting my gaze again with some sort of resolved look.

Getting to my feet, I held out a hand to help her up. "I think we should call it a night. It's already after one," I said, looking to my watch which read twelve after the hour.

"You'll hear no argument from me." She smiled. "I think I could sleep for a week and still want to nap midday."

. . .

At around two thirty, I was finally succumbing to my exhaustion, after having left Jana at her bedroom door with a sweet goodnight kiss, when something stirred me awake.

I struggled through sleepiness to figure out what had woken me when a small gentle hand landed on my bare chest.

Jana.

"Go back to sleep," she whispered, cuddling into my side with far too much bare skin, which had my body tingling from head to toe.

Ignoring my body's response, my eyes having adjusted to the dark bedroom, I cleared my throat. "Everything okay?"

"Yeah," she sighed, then amended. "No. I got to my room, and as exhausted as I feel, I couldn't get back to sleep."

Moving to wrap an arm around her, bringing her in closer to my side where she was forced to lean her head on my shoulder, I buffed my cheek against the crown of her head, taking in the delicate peach scent of her shampoo. "S'okay."

Delivering a quick peck to my chest, I felt her body melt and relax into mine. "I didn't want to be alone."

Covering the hand at my stomach, I squeezed. "Stay. I want you to stay."

And I meant the single word wholeheartedly as I closed my eyes, relishing the feel of this woman who had me tied in knots.

Stay for tonight. Tomorrow. Into next week.

Forever, was the final thought that occurred as darkness took me.

JANA

It had taken Brycen a few minutes to succumb to slumber last night, and nearly another twenty minutes of my watching the minutes tick by on his bedside clock before I could put the fact I needed him at my side at all to sleep peacefully.

I was used to going at it alone.

I've never needed anyone.

Until now.

It wasn't until the early hours this morning, I was ready to acknowledge having him made the burden that was my life, at the present, easier to bear. And what was more, if I truly looked past all the shit that was my exes, my mother's relationship with my father, the one-nighter habit Jason had adopted over the years, and so many countless other relationships I'd witness crash and burn, I *knew*.

I knew Brycen wasn't like the others.

I knew whatever pulled at us was ultimately different from every other time before.

I knew this was what everyone strived for—a lover, a friend —a partner in life.

And if I was smart, I'd give in to the man's support, take his strength, embrace it even, give it all back to him in spades, and see where this all went between us.

It wasn't until those early morning hours I realized—while reveling in the heat of his body against mine—that Brycen had held on to me throughout the entire night, offering wordless security and warmth, and I was convinced I'd be crazy to run from *this*.

With an urgency I'd never felt before now, I had to see where life would take me—take *us*.

And if it didn't work out?

Well, I'd most likely be shredded beyond repair, but I couldn't think about that.

"I've never had another woman in this house, never mind my bedroom." He had me jumping.

Instead of acknowledging this factoid, I led with, "You're awake."

"Mmm," he said into the top of my head, buffing his cheek against my hair. His hand began a slow caress over my back, up to my shoulders, never stopping. "Slept like the dead," he rasped. "How 'bout you?"

His question had me assessing my state of being, and I was surprised at how I felt. My mind was clearer this morning, and the weight I'd become accustomed to, which seemed to make me feel like every muscle in my body was filled with lead, had dissipated considerably.

"You're smiling," his sleep-roughened baritone had my body warming, wondering what that tone would feel like as he spoke all sorts of nonsense against other parts of my body, because the utter vibration of his voice against my cheek had me thinking so many impure thoughts.

"Uhm." I struggled to find my words, but he was quicker.

"Need the bathroom?" His humored words had me realizing I'd clenched my legs, rubbing my thighs slightly to quell the building heat in my core. My stomach did a somersault, and the butterflies went aflutter.

With my most recent decision to give in to our mutual attraction being so fresh, it felt embarrassing to be talking about these types of biological responses, so to let him know I wasn't in need of the toilet, I set to thank the man for all he'd done for me—for my family—thus far.

As I peppered his bare chest with open-mouthed kisses, occasionally alternating between gentle nips and licks, reveling in his low groans, and the increase in his breathing, Brycen broke the erotic silence with, "I take it that's a no," before he flipped us over, smiling down at me.

The weight of his body, his legs on the outside of mine, cocooning me into his heat had me melting into the bed with a moan while his eyes drank me in. Our hands and fingers were interlocked on either side of my pillowed head. I was fully pinned and surrounded by this man, and I couldn't think of anywhere else I wanted to be right then.

The man's gaze narrowed when I arched my hips into his on another moan.

"Jesus, woman." His eyes turned to molten chocolate, almost black in the dim lighting of the bedroom, thanks to what must have been blackout shades. "You're making it hard to keep my hands off of you."

Digging into my no-longer-so-dormant inner vixen, I grinned, all the while keeping my gaze locked on him. *All in*, I repeated internally, and said, "Then don't." I punctuated the sureness of my statement, request, demand...hell, I'd beg him if it led to that, by arching my head up and capturing his mouth with mine until I'd had him as drugged on lust as he had me with the sheer weight of him, and my inability to physically escape him in that moment.

BRYCEN

All systems go, my brain shouted, and damn, what with her already naked flesh beneath mine, it was a miracle I hadn't blown my load prematurely as soon as our lower torsos made contact. And that kiss...

Having enough brainpower to pull away, I nuzzled her nose, then peered down at her. "You're sure?"

Shifting so her legs opened, and I fell toward the heat of her center, she nodded. "I've never been any surer about wanting someone like I do you."

I closed my eyes and allowed her sincerity to soak in.

Her quick kiss to the side of my mouth had me looking at her once more. "Make me forget, Brycen. Make me yours."

Well, fuck!

twenty-one

JANA

"MAKE ME YOURS," I said. And as quick as apprehension reared its ugly head for making myself so vulnerable, it vanished in point-five seconds.

Because Brycen's hands released mine and set about roaming.

Because his thick cock, based on the feel of it against my naked thigh, throbbed in time as his large hands trailed the inside of my arms, leaving a path of goosebumps in their wake as he cupped one of my breasts.

And because his mouth turned every bit of skin it touched into an erogenous zone I could have never guessed I'd possessed until this morning.

My God, if the man fucked as great as he kissed, I was about to be propelled into nirvana, and would most likely not care if I returned.

A flick of a tongue against my nipple had me latching a hand behind his head to hold him to my cleavage, making the vibration of his groan around the peak tauten.

"Fuck," he growled, "my baby's so responsive."

A brief laugh escaped me, making him look up and meet my eyes, an arched brow in question.

"Your baby hasn't had cock in over two years," I blurted. "I wasn't kidding when I said I could come from your kisses alone yesterday."

The man grinned, and those dimples of his popped out. "I've been dying to test that theory since you mentioned it," he confessed. "Why don't we give it an honest to goodness try, huh?"

The nod I gave him came without thought, and I retorted, "You need to put your mouth where your words are, buster."

Laughing, he lifted himself slightly, dipping his mouth to my breastbone, all the while holding my gaze. "Don't worry, sweetheart, by the time I'm done with you, you'll be begging for me to leave you alone."

I doubt it, I thought to myself as he proceeded to trail his tongue to my navel, playing around the soft skin there, making me quiver, so I closed my eyes and relaxed into his more than capable hands.

Surely, I'd never survive when he got to...

"Brycen! Shit!"

My back bowed off the mattress as soon as he fused his mouth to my clit and sucked.

The vibration of his deep laugh had liquid pooling between my thighs.

"Fuck, yeah," he growled, the width of a thick digit breaching my entrance, "you're soaked."

Inserting a second finger, he fused his lips to my nub, gracing it with a few flicks of his tongue as his fingers hit something magical that would have had me levitate off the mattress had his other arm not been holding me down. I liquified at how full I felt.

"Jesus! Fuck!" I clawed at the sheets on either side of me, my hips gyrating as if they had a mind of their own.

"That's it, baby," he crooned, licking my slit from bottom to top. "You're fucking hot. Delicious. Make yourself come on my hand and mouth."

The filth of his language only incited the burning in my body until reality came crashing down.

Freezing, I lifted my head to look down at him, my eyes narrowing. "Not without you, I'm not. I can't." I bit my bottom lip, pushing forth with my admission. "I can't come more than once, and I want you inside me when I do this first time."

The man had the decency to look vexed, meeting my gaze with a look of determination, a cocky smirk gracing his glistening lips.

"I ought to beat the shit out of every man who left you wanting and convinced that this can only happen once a session, baby."

"But—"

The single determined shake of his head and the look of warning that brooked no argument in his eyes shut me right up.

BRYCEN

Fucking jackasses, I thought as soon as Jana confessed she'd never been able to come more than once in a single romp.

I felt humbled that she trusted me enough to be honest, and I knew, if I pushed, she'd probably confess that she'd not always been taken care of or reached release every time with a partner.

"But—"

With a singular shake of my head, I shut her up. *That's about to change,* I conveyed with my eyes before I leaned down to feast on her juices.

Damn, but with every lick and suck, it was as if I was tasting her for the very first time. Sweet. Warm. Sinfully sexy.

I could worship at the altar of Jana every damn day for the rest of my life, if she'd allow it, and die a happy man.

My cock twitched nonstop, and to ease some of the ache I

felt, I ground myself into the mattress, hoping what little friction I achieved aided in providing subtle relief. At least, until it was time for me to make her mine.

As soon as my fingers felt the tiny flutters of her heated folds, I knew I had her right where I wanted her.

Flexing my digits so the pads hit the subtle bumpy surface inside her, Jana's hand reached and clutched at my hair at a nearly painful level, and an "Oh my God! Brycen, yes!" pierced my ears. Her heat clenched onto me as more juices flowed with her orgasm, and I lapped her up.

As she descended from the stratosphere, I proceeded to ease her down with one final light lick to her folds to satiate my hunger for her on my taste buds.

When her hand eased its grip, I collapsed to the bed beside her, taking in her expression of bliss, the subtle sheen of sweat over her exposed chest, and I couldn't wait any longer.

Jana

Holy Christ on a crutch! I thought as I came back from my orgasmic stupor to find a Grecian god up on his knees between my thighs. Another surge of lust took me over as he sheathed himself with a condom I had no recollection of him acquiring.

As he fisted his length a few times, his eyes never leaving my face, I swear that the ebbing aftershocks of my previous orgasm ramped up again, and need like none I'd ever felt before so soon after an epic orgasm took hold.

Brycen proceeded to lean down, kissing up my navel, to my breastbone, over my shoulder as he eased his weight over me, eliciting a full body shiver from me at the wholistic contact.

The man's sweet smile captured me, his body held me, and his cock, nudging my heat, was about to possess me.

One second, he was breaching my entrance, and in the next

instant, he surged forward, fusing his mouth to mine, capturing my cry of pained bliss.

Damn, but he was huge.

"Eyes on me," Brycen rasped, his lips feathering light kisses across my cheekbones.

His fingers tickled the side of my face, coming away damp, and the tenderness of the gesture, let alone his expression, had the remnants of the ice surrounding my heart, and whatever may have remained of my pessimism, melt away as though it had never existed.

"Too much?" he asked, the tightness to his lips alluding to the fact that he was struggling to control his baser instincts to rut like an animal.

"No." Shuddering in a breath, I tilted my head to kiss the inside of the wrist that was by my face, keeping his eyes and added, "Perfect." Then I leaned up to capture his lips in a long, slow, drugging kiss before pulling away, wrapping my arms around him. "Hurts so good." Brycen's forehead dropped as he chuckled against my shoulder. "But if you don't start moving soon, I'm gonna have to hurt you."

This had him in full belly laughs, cut short on a drawn-out groan because I clenched around his girth, enunciating my demand.

"Damn, baby," he punctuated his words by withdrawing his hips, then surging forth again. "This is going to be fast. I promise to make it up to you next time."

"Promises, promises."

twenty-two

Jana

MULTIPLES. What a wonderful concept!

Brycen hadn't lied when he said it was going to be a quick round, but what neither of us expected was the monster orgasm that surged through me when I'd urged him to get moving. From his first thrust, his thickness stroked some undiscovered spot inside that had me breaking records, detonating to the point I took him over the edge with me.

After another one of his sweet kisses, Brycen pulled away, smiling down at me.

"I've gotta get rid of this rubber." He kissed me again. "Don't move."

As he liberated himself from the sheets, I rolled to my side and my eyes perused the width and musculature of his shoulders, down to his arms. And when my sight landed on his sculpted ass, I heard myself groaning. It was a fucking work of art.

After a toilet flush, the sink running next, Brycen came strutting back.

Is it wrong that I want you again so soon?

"Give me half an hour," he said as he started to crawl back into bed, then looked down at his mostly flaccid dick, which twitched with more life than he evidently expected, what with the surprised expression on his face which had him grinning. "The things you do to me, woman," he mumbled against the top of my head after I'd draped myself over his chest.

"Ditto," I punctuated that with a kiss over his sternum, settling in against him.

"Hello!" I heard from the kitchen as Brycen and I were preparing brunch, followed by Bailey skittering on the kitchen tile as he attempted a mad dash toward the front of the house.

"Shit," he cursed, shooting me a panicked look as another woman said, "Mom, didn't you learn anything about barging into homes without knocking first when you caught Brent and I—"

"Oh pish, Rebecca. Your brother told me he was working today," the lady said, then added a, "Well, hello!" when a mid-to-late-sixties woman came barreling to a halt in the kitchen with loads of bags in both her hands, Brycen's dog circling around her.

"Mom!" another woman scolded, as another one came to a stop beside her. Her eyes widened when they took in the over-sized man's button-down shirt I was dressed in. The look of shock dissipated within seconds when her closed fist over her lips attempted to cover up her humor, which was useless considering the nervous giggle that came burbling out.

If I had to guess, despite their short stature, these three had to be Brycen's mother and two of his sisters. The eyes, hair color, and overall resemblant stunning looks were more than enough to prove it.

I couldn't be any more embarrassed.

Brycen

As soon as Mom came into the kitchen, I rushed around to my visitors' side of the island, thankful that even though Jana was in nothing but her skimpy underwear and one of my dress shirts—which has never looked any better, I might add—that the counter would block the sight of her endless bare legs, so long as she stayed right where she was.

As soon as I heard Coraline's giggle, however, I knew the jig was up, and it was only going to be a matter of time before Rebecca clued in.

"Mom." I smiled at the tiny spitfire who had raised me, then proceeded to give her a hug, looking at Rebecca and adding, "Becks, I thought you stole the key from her the last time she caught you and Brent getting it on."

She shrugged. "I thought she'd learn to knock after she caught me with my husband's dick in my mouth. I was wrong."

I groaned; these are things a brother could go a lifetime without hearing about. "Thanks for that image, sis. Not sure there's enough bleach in the world to purge that from my mind."

Jana tried to cover her shocked gasp with a soft cough at my sister's unashamed and too-much-information level statement.

"Well, at least the second time you had it right." I released my mother as she continued talking, "I love my grandbabies, but there's no way you can give me anymore when you're swallowing that man's magic juice."

These women were just too much sometimes—even for me.

A hiccupped giggle punctuated the air from behind me.

Pinching the bridge of my nose, I shook my head, terrified to turn and look at my houseguest. I wouldn't have been shocked if Jana ran out of here like her hair had caught fire in the next five minutes if the other women in my life kept carrying on the way they were.

"Becks," I said, giving my oldest sister a hug, then moving to

Cora to give her hers, before rushing back to help my mother with the shopping bags.

"Well, who do we have here?" Mom asked as soon as I relieved her of her burden, turning to set everything on the island countertop and finding a wide-eyed, blushing Jana.

"Working, my ass," Rebecca muttered under her breath from right behind me.

"Shut up, Becks," I rumbled quietly, then proceeded to our mother's side, guiding all three of them to the stools on the opposite side of the island to have a seat. "Mom, Becks, Cora, this is Jana," I introduced.

"Hallelujah!" Cora exclaimed as I made my way to stand behind Jana, ready to support her through this unplanned and, albeit, awkward first meeting.

Next thing I knew, Mom flew around the island, coming at a dead stop right in front of my woman—it didn't matter that we hadn't labeled things—before pulling her away from me, and wrapping her in her arms as if she'd known her forever.

"I can't believe it's finally happened!" She giggled, shaking Jana from side to side, ensuring the much taller woman to hold on to the force of nature who was my mother just to stay on her feet.

I braced myself for an overwhelmed Jana, but the smile she graced me with, once my mother had released her, was a sweet one. Then, she surprised me further by leaving my side and jumping into things with both feet.

"Tell me truly," she said in a conspiring tone, smirking at me before she leaned an elbow onto the island, cradling her chin in her hand, "did you girls seriously use him as your baby doll growing up?"

I sniggered as Rebecca and Coraline looked at one another with matching grins before turning to Jana with twin nods and Coraline jumped in to expand.

"Dressed him up, did his hair, and—"

"Ha!" Mom harrumphed as she nudged me toward Jana,

taking the creamer and milk bottles I'd just grabbed from one of the bags from my hands, and began stowing away the groceries they'd brought, as she added, "You two begged your father and me to let his hair grow so you could braid it!"

"He had such beautiful hair," Coraline added all dreamlike.

"But we had to make do with those barrettes," Becks finished. "Mom contemplated it for all but a few seconds before Dad put the kibosh on it all."

Jana smiled up at me before leaning into my arm, which I moved to wrap around her shoulders, bringing her closer. "I'm gonna have to see pictures, you know that, right?"

"I'm sure I have one around here somewhere," I confessed before pressing my lips to the hairline next to her ear.

"Aw!" Rebecca swooned.

"You two are so sweet," Coraline added. "You should come to Sunday dinner."

To everyone else, Jana might have looked like she simply rolled with my sister's words, but I felt the subtle bit of tension that shuddered through her body before her face flushed with a blush and she relaxed into me once more.

"Yes, dear." Mom came up to her other side, and when I turned, she'd already managed to put everything away, even the grocery bags were nowhere to be seen. "I've been waiting a good long time for this day."

"Mom," I cautioned.

Instead, she patted Jana's hand, gaining her attention. "Now, Jana, don't you dare feel obligated," Mom started with a reassuring smile. "I know we're a bit much, but we're just so excited to finally meet someone who means something to our Brycen."

"T-thank you?" she stuttered.

"What they're trying to say," I interrupted, turning Jana so she faced me, "is that I've never brought anyone home until now."

She gave a curt nod. "Yeah, you've mentioned that."

"And he's never let us meet anybody either," Coraline added softly.

Blushing, she shrugged her shoulders, smirking shyly at me. "Not like I could have gone anywhere in this."

Rebecca giggled. "Nah, he'd have found somewhere for you to hole up until we'd cleared the property if he was against us meeting you."

"Becks." I tried to bestow a reprimanding glare on my sister, but Jana's snicker had me grinning down at her instead.

"How about we get out of your hair, and you can think on it," Mom suggested.

Jana slowly turned and met each of my sisters' excitedly hopeful gazes before she turned to face my mother and nodded. "I'll think about it. Promise."

Then, she did something that shocked me as much as it seemed to have shocked my mother. She stepped forward, leaned to kiss my mom's cheek, and by the time her arms came up to hug her, Mom already had her in her grasp.

Sneaking a look to my sisters, it seemed we were a little surprised about this turn of events, but my siblings' smiles were encouraging, and the smile Mom shot me as she pulled me down to give my cheek a big smacking kiss left me feeling optimistic because every one of their smiles, boasted their unofficial seal of approval.

twenty-three

JANA

A WEEK WENT by in a flash with Brycen and I falling into some sort of a routine. It was nice, but in all honesty, I was bored shitless. Aside from Mom's doctor's appointments, we hadn't left Brycen's house. My only saving grace was that I had a new best friend in Bailey, who refused to leave my side while Brycen put in some hours for NSI. Between bouts of fetch, running around the backyard as we chased one another, I had also put quite the sizeable dent in my lengthy Kindle list of to-be-reads.

Sure, I'd kept myself busy by maintaining much of Brycen's home, which wasn't much as the man seemed to have a complex about keeping things clean and tidy, so that meant that aside from the occasional bout of dishes for two, and a couple of loads of laundry every few days, there'd been nothing much to do aside from take up cooking duties.

Which is what brought me to Brycen's office.

"Smoked meat on rye, coming at ya," I announced, letting myself in.

Spinning in his chair to face me, the man smiled while

holding up a finger. "Yeah, I got it," he spoke into the headset he was wearing. "Thanks, Huss," he added before his arm snapped out, grabbed on to the front of my shirt, pulling me so I had nowhere to go as I landed on his lap, straddling him. He'd done this every time I'd come to him—always showering me with attention—even when he was otherwise engaged in his work. "Yeah," he said, as he relieved my hands from the plateful of sandwich and plain chips I'd piled on, depositing it onto the corner of his desk. "Uh-huh," he confirmed, then leaned in to press his lips against mine before pulling away far enough for me to see the gleam in his eyes. "Yeah, I'll let her know. Okay, right. Bye."

In a fraction of a second, the man shed his headset, flinging it over his shoulder as it landed on the desk behind him, no concern for anything, or anyone, other than me. Grabbing my face in his hands, he slammed his mouth onto mine, his tongue immediately demanding entrance.

And I gave it to him.

By the time he released me, I was squirming against his lap, greedily looking for a way to quell the ache in my core.

"My baby made me food again," he rumbled, tucking a strand of hair behind my ear, then nuzzled my nose with his. "You know you don't have to."

Cupping his cheek with one hand, then wrapping the other arm around his shoulders, I nipped at his bottom lip, then said, "I know, but I feel like I need to do something more than keep house and sit on my ass all day."

A hand reached said ass, squeezing my left cheek. "I like your ass, Jana. I love squeezing it." He punctuated the next series of words with a kiss. "It's a great handful to hold on to when I'm fucking you into the mattress. The way it jiggles when I do you from behind makes me want to bite into those juicy globes. And when you let me touch you *there*, the way your pussy grips my cock is unlike anything I've ever experienced."

"Christ, Brycen." I swallowed hard, squirming some more. "I think you just disintegrated my underwear with your words."

He chuckled. "You like it when I talk dirty?" His hands reached for the hem of my shirt, working it up above my boobs. Then he shifted his seat so we turned and I was forced to brace my arms on the edge of his desk, as he peppered kisses and nips across my cleavage before he settled his nose between my tits, taking a long inhale.

Sure, I could bitch and moan about being bored, but for the last week, these sexy interludes, and quality time with Brycen were what I lived for.

"I can't wait to fuck these," he rumbled, pinching a nipple through my lacy bra, the sting making me hiss.

"Yesss," I pleaded. "Anything."

"Anything?" He pulled back, his eyes connecting with mine and all I could do was nod.

When his grin came out to play, dimples and all, I couldn't help myself and leaned in to lick one of them.

With a hard squeeze of both ass cheeks, he demanded, "Up you go, baby. Turn around, face the desk, and bend over."

A bolt of heat zinged to my nether regions, and I felt myself liquify. "In here?" *Please let it be here.*

"Fuck yeah," he rasped, then reached for my leggings, pulling them down to my ankles as he hissed at the sight I evidently made. "Thought you said you were wearing underwear, baby." I heard the telltale thump of his knees hitting the floor behind me and felt his hands at my ankles, guiding me to lift my right foot so he could release it from the pantleg. He didn't bother with the other, simply gliding his calloused hands up the back of my calves, tapping at the backs of my knees. "Spread for me, Jana," he said before depositing a nip to the back of my left thigh. "I need to taste you."

A moan escaped me the moment his finger traced the crack of my butt, settling to circle the rosette a few times before he held me open, and the warmth of his breath shuddered over my heat.

His moan at his first taste of me had me nearly falling over the precipice. "Fuck, I could spend days doing just this, Jana. This is all I'd need to survive this life." He flicked his tongue against my nub and pressed three fingers inside of me, hitting that magic spot he seemed so well-versed in locating, and it was all too much.

My knees shook, my pulse thrummed in my head, my vision dimmed, and the breath in my chest rattled as Brycen held me up for fear that I'd collapse as he buried his face into me, licking at me through my orgasm, until I was firmly on the other side of the crest.

Within moments, I felt his bare chest against my back, and his cock at my entrance.

"Fuck, baby," he gritted out, "you're so fucking tight like this."

My eyes rolled into the back of my head as his girth stretched me to the edge of pleasure and pain. "You're so big."

"You say such sweet things." He chuckled and bit my shoulder before he wrapped his arms around me, a hand trailing to my pussy, the other up to gently surround my neck, tilting my face so he could get to my lips.

"Fuck me, Brycen," I urged by tilting my ass so he could get in deeper.

"As the lady wishes," he ground out.

And he set a pace that led to mutually assured gratification.

BRYCEN

"Let me know when you're ready to come home." I moved into Jana, pressing her against Dalton's front door.

Rubbing her cheek against the scruff of mine, she whispered, "I could have driven myself over here." Her hands smoothed over my chest.

"You know I can't do that, sweetheart." My fingers played with the edge of her shirt, the tips feathering light caresses over the soft skin of her torso. "First, because there's a psycho out there looking for you, and second…" I nipped at her lips. "You can let your hair down, relax, and enjoy those lemon drops I know are waiting for you behind that door. You deserve to unwind and not have to worry about anyone else but you." I kissed her then, urging her lips open to get a taste of her sweetness, making her moan.

"Hey, when you're done mauling her, let yourselves in." D chuckled through the doorbell microphone.

"Oh, my God," Jana groaned, burying her face in my chest while my shoulders shook with my humor, "this is—"

Tucking my thumb under her chin, I guided her face upward, so her eyes met mine, and grinned. "Perfect? Right? Meant to be?"

She shrugged, the tilt of her lips deepening to a grin to match my own. "I was going to say embarrassing, but you know what?" She pecked the side of my jaw.

"What, baby?"

Her expression sobered from the humor that was just there, but her gaze softened on mine. "This does feel right, Brycen," she whispered before pressing her lips to mine, my heart skipped a beat, then began racing at the sheer honesty of her statement.

Thank fuck I wasn't the only one to feel that way. Christ, I was more than halfway in love with her after having her living with me for a little over a week.

twenty-four

Jana

"HOLY SHIT!" Devolin mumbled after Brycen, Dalton, Shane, Theo, and Cade had left the house.

"That was—" what sounded like Morgan started.

"Hot, with an h-a-w-t, hot," Aspen supplied as I tried to regain my footing after the toe-curling kiss Brycen had delivered before his departure.

Emberlyn simply giggled, and when I turned around, heat suffusing my face, the wide-eyed looks from all three women had me grinning like I was the cat who'd gotten the canary right before we all dissolved into a fit of giggles.

Lemon drop numero dos had just been decimated and Devolin promptly got to her feet, rushing for the kitchen island with her empty pitcher, readying to mix another batch for all of us.

"Don't stop on my account," she called as she began to pour the vodka, spilling over the measuring cup she was using. If she kept it up, we'd all be hurting come morning.

Emberlyn's excited nod urged me to continue, and the enthralled look from Aspen—not to mention the alcohol coursing through my veins—had me spilling about the hot office interlude Brycen and I had indulged in the day before, albeit, with some censorship. There were just some things that were best kept between a couple.

"You oughta put that in a book, Aspen," Devolin stated as she collapsed in her seat after having refilled everyone's glass.

The other woman grinned. "What makes you think I haven't already?"

"Bitch, I've read you, and you have *not* written anything similar to that in the one office romance you published," Devolin stated, both Morgan and Emberlyn met each other's gazes, then busted a gut laughing.

My brows furrowed as I bit my lip. "What are you guys going on about?" I asked, entirely confused.

"Ever hear of Penny Sexton?" Emberlyn asked, excitement making me edgy as she bounced on the edge of her seat.

"Well, yeah, who hasn't?" I shrugged, meeting each pair of eyes in the room until my gaze froze on Aspen, whose grin widened as she lifted her hand, wiggling her fingers in a *hey there* manner.

Proffering her hand to me, she giggled and proceeded to blow my mind. "Penny Sexton," she said, lifting her martini glass in a *cheers* gesture.

What?

"Oh, Lord," Morgan said as she collapsed into the back of the couch with hilarity. "Look at her!"

My head spun, and I was pretty sure it had more to do with the bomb these women had dropped on me than the alcohol I'd ingested so far.

"Is she gonna faint?" Morgan asked the room.

Breathe, must catch breath. Don't make a scene just because book royalty is sitting across the room from you, Jana.

Before anyone could say anything else, I had managed to compose myself enough to ever so eloquently say, "You're shitting me, right?"

The woman in question graced me with a warm smile, which evolved into a Cheshire grin. "Nope, but you now have a new best friend who's going to want to pick your brain about that 9-1-1 gig of yours. And if you just so happen to provide me with some juicy, hanky-panky tidbits, you can damn well bet your sexy ass I'll be adding my own flair to that too."

"Oh shit, Dev, looks like you're not the only one who's being written about now," Emberlyn announced to the room at large.

Huh? Then I remembered reading the few sample chapters of Penny Sexton's latest romantic suspense, which was scheduled to release next month—something about a hacker.

Taking a healthy gulp of my drink—okay, I may have drained the entire bottom half of my glass—I looked at Devolin, shook my head with subtle disbelief still present, and stated, "Not sure Brycen would be on par with Aspen writing about us, and I can't imagine a man like Dalton would have been okay with that."

Devolin smirked as Aspen giggled. "I didn't write their story, silly! I merely modeled a few characters after them—their jobs mostly. And if a few bits of D's growliness made it into the book, it would only make the read that much better. The grumpy-sunshine trope is all the rage these days. Everyone loves a man with a sexy growl every now and again. Add to that an alpha domineering quality, and bam! Total hotness."

"Although..." Devolin paused to take a sip of her drink. "You know that scene when Jaxon bound Shelly with her clothes, leaving her at his mercy, then shamelessly fucked her when anyone could have walked in on them?"

My brows rose to my hairline at the hot picture my mind made up. "That's no scene I've read yet," I mumbled.

"Hold on! I got it!" Morgan got up and ran for her purse.

"It's time we properly indoctrinated Jana to the clan." She came back with her Kindle in hand as she hurriedly tapped at the screen, then handed it to me. "Read this. I've already cued up Chapter Seventeen for you."

Taking it from her, I looked at the screen, only to see it's the one and only book I haven't yet read of Penny's—aka Aspen's—simply because it hadn't been published yet.

"Go for it," Aspen encouraged, the others sitting back with their drinks, not saying a word, but silently urging me to go on. "I'll send you the entire manuscript after I get home tonight, then you can tell me what you think."

Five minutes later, I closed my eyes, trying to avoid from squirming in my seat, thanks to what I'd just read, then cleared my throat as I handed the Kindle back to Morgan. But that's as far as I got before I broke.

"Dalton is a naughty, naughty man!" I giggled.

"Blame her," Devolin pointed to Aspen. "She wrote it, and my man desperately had to ensure a certain degree of quality assurance. Unbeknownst to me, the bugger was reading the book whenever I wasn't. I can't help that he read ahead of where I was, then surprised me with that—"

"How come I'm only hearing about this now?" Aspen pouted. "You've had the book for like two months!"

"Oh, my God!" Morgan jumped up, covering her mouth. "It was you!" Devolin blushed. "Last month's family barbecue! In the barn?"

"You got an audio?" Aspen blurted, Emberlyn beside herself with giggles.

Morgan nodded. "Heard a lot before I got my ass out of there. At first, I thought it was Paxton and his wife—my brother-in-law—because they have this fucked-up habit of sometimes running off with one another for some alone time.

Alyssa said they did it because it kept things spicy." She drank up the remainder of her drink, then set her empty martini glass on the coffee table. "All I can say is that it sounded like someone was getting it good and proper. Hell, what I heard had me so riled up, it's why I rushed Theo out of there just so we could go home and get it on, especially knowing his parents had the baby. I just assumed it was them."

The room broke out in giggles, me included.

"I fail to see how I caused a problem in all of this." Aspen attempted a demure sip, but faltered. Instead, she sputtered the final drink from her glass as a fit of giggles hit her. I handed her one of the cocktail napkins next to the charcuterie board as she nodded her thanks, while she proceeded to mop at her chin and the front of her shirt.

Plucking an olive off the tray and shoving it into my mouth, I added, "Sounds to me like everyone had a *really* great night." Everyone else broke into cheers, taking turns high-fiving Devolin.

I'd never truly felt at home with other groups of women before. Except for my two best girls—Reina and Jess—I hadn't realized what I'd been missing until now. The link to these ladies went beyond sharing men who were friends and worked with one another. We were kindred spirits in so many ways that these women—even those I'd only met tonight—had brought me into the fold and made me one of them.

Brycen had brought so much more with him into our relationship than I could have ever imagined: family, friendship, a sense of belonging, safety—and love. To say I loved Brycen would have been jumping the proverbial gun a little, but I knew I was falling, and so long as I didn't get in my way, I knew it would inevitably happen. And I planned to embrace it with all that I was when it eventually became reality.

BRYCEN

164

"Fuck me," Cade mumbled under his breath, a small miracle I even heard him over the music as I brought up the rear to our group of men. Tate and Rex had both been keeping an eye on the house, but both men were absent from their vehicles when we arrived, which had me worried.

"Your wife did it again, D, and your girl is fitting right in." Theo laughed as he clapped me on the shoulder, making room after I'd brought up the rear of our group.

My apprehension was quick to subside when we cleared the front entrance, and I found the two men on watch duty grinning at us.

Genuine's "Pony" blared from someone's phone plugged into the docking station that sat on the living room's side table, while a tremendous amount of giggling ensued. The five of us men settled in for the show.

Aspen, Emberlyn, and Morgan surrounded red-faced and sputtering Devolin and Jana as the three standing women bumped and ground to the best of their ability. Their moves were clumsy, most likely due to the empty martini glasses and God only knew how many times the half-empty pitcher that sat on the coffee table had been refilled.

"I wonder how long it'll take for them to clue in we're here," Shane said just as Jana started making imaginary money rain for the twerking triplets, Devolin sticking her fingers in her mouth to cat call whistle at the women before the two toppled over one another on the couch, another fit of giggles taking over.

"I don't know, but it seems like they might be hurting come tomorrow," Tate stated, shaking his head with a smirk. "We've been standing here for nearly ten minutes, and they still haven't noticed."

Next thing we knew, Aspen turned around and paused mid-twerk before a grin split her face right before she rushed for Cade, throwing herself, sure the man would catch her—which he did—right before she laid a sloppy kiss on him.

"I have a feeling you're partly behind all of this," Cade rumbled against his fiancée's neck.

"I plead the Fifth, handsome. Now take me home so I can show you my moves," she demanded, making Tate and Rex crack up.

Next up, Theo located his wife's purse, grabbed it, then made his way to her, spinning her around, then threw her over his shoulder, smacking her ass as he made for the door. "Later, everybody. Seems I've got a date with a hellion."

"Keep out of barns," Emberlyn called out as Shane bent to kiss her giggling mouth. Theo barely paused in his retreat, but I didn't miss the blush on Dalton's face as both men's gazes connected for a split second.

I wonder what that was about.

When Shane and Ember bid us goodbye, Tate and Rex took their leave as Dalton headed for the phone on the docking station, bringing the music to a silent halt.

"Aw! Just when it was our turn to bust a move," Devolin grumped unconvincingly, thanks to the smirk on her face. She tried to get up to greet her husband, but toppled over backward onto the couch, this inducing another fit of giggles between Jana and herself.

Dalton simply shook his head, grin firmly in place, as I approached and took a knee in front of a collapsed Jana.

Swiping the strands of hair that covered her face, I smiled. "You're cute when you're drunk," I said.

"And you're hot," she blurted, then a look of excitement crossed her eyes, and she hurriedly sat up. "Aspen is writing a book about us," she announced. "We were working out a scene. That's why we were dancing." Her brows furrowed like she struggled to remember the night's events. "I think." Then her lips made an O. "Oh! And Dalton fucked Devolin in the barn!"

"Christ," Dalton mumbled as he pinched the bridge of his nose, then looked to his wife, but Jana kept on going before he could say anything.

"It's Aspen's fault, honestly. She really shouldn't write such steamy books, although…" She paused, then grinned at me. "I think I have her sold on writing a scene just like what we did yesterday. You know, when you made me turn around, then you—"

And we're done here. I covered Jana's mouth before she went into far too much detail about yesterday's foray in my home office in front of our friends, although I was pretty sure I was too late for that in any case.

"Let's get you home, sweetheart," I said, then pulled my hand from her mouth, ensuring her silence by pressing my mouth to hers in a brief kiss.

"Mmm," she whispered against my lips. "Please take me home, Brycen. My ladies and I have had a rather illuminating night, and I'm aching to have you fuck—"

On a chuckle, joined by both Dalton and Devolin's laughs, I slapped my hand over Jana's mouth again, and shook my head to silence her once more. "Tell me in the car, now let's get out of here."

She grabbed my hand and let me pull her up to her feet and toward the front door. "Talk Monday," I said as Jana looked back to Devolin, who demanded, "Call me tomorrow. I want to know what you think. Love you, babe!"

"You too, Dev," she called out before I shut the front door and hurried us to the car.

"Think about what?" I asked her as soon as I buckled myself into the driver's seat.

"Aspen's latest book." I spotted the hungry gaze on her face, thanks to the illuminated dashboard, just as her hand came to land on my upper thigh, slowly moving toward my crotch.

"Christ," I cursed. "Baby, hold that thought. We're about five minutes from home."

She sighed, sounding so bereft. "If you say so, but I was hoping to have a snack on the way." Her eyes met mine.

"Jesus, woman," I breathed, understanding her meaning.

"Not tonight, baby. The first time I get that hot mouth of yours around my cock, I want to be fully in the moment, not trying to avoid curbs and oncoming traffic while I hurry us home."

And hurry us home I damn well fucking did.

twenty-five

BRYCEN

AS SOON AS Bailey had been let out and tended to, I gave him the command to head for his bed, which he'd obeyed straightaway, while I headed toward my bedroom.

When I entered the room, I damn well nearly swallowed my tongue at what I found—naked and kneeling on the floor at the foot of my bed.

She was beautiful.

Sexy as sin.

And all mine.

Crooking her finger for me to approach her, wearing nothing but a sultry smile, she immediately reached for the button of my fly as soon as I was within reaching distance, and pulled me the rest of the way before pausing so our eyes connected.

"I want to make you feel good." She proceeded with unzipping my pants, then snuck her hands around and into the back of my jeans, pushing them down past my hips as she shoved her nose into my groin before blowing a puff of air through my boxer briefs and onto my cock. "I want to taste you on my tongue." She rushed at helping me step out of the denim, pulling my socks off as she went. "And I want to swallow you whole after you fuck my mouth." Her hands pulled my underwear down, releasing me as I gulped down the sudden urge to possess her then and there.

If she looked at me like that any longer, I'd blow my load before we even began.

The moment her hand surrounded my length at the root, I hissed and her grip tightened.

The pink of her tongue took a tentative lick, tracing the slit at the top of my head before she sucked at the tip of me.

"Jana." I swallowed, my hand feathering through her hair, cupping the back of her head gently.

She pulled back, tracing the veins in my length with her tongue, while her other hand lightly massaged my balls, before sinking her mouth down on me as far as she could take my cock.

"Holy shit!" I blurted out as she fought her gag reflex, breathing through her nose, and my length bumped the back of her throat. "Baby, you suck so good."

She pulled back slightly, humming her response, and the telltale tingle of a monster orgasm prickled at the base of my spine.

"If you want me to fuck your face, baby, this is going to be quick," I panted, gritting my teeth against her onslaught, "and it's gonna have to be now."

Jana's eyes went completely molten, and her efforts seemed to double as soon as I began shallow thrusts into her mouth.

The moment her finger massaged the space between my sac and asshole, she broke me.

"I'm fucking coming for you, baby," I growled. "You're so fucking hot. Take me, take my cum. Shit! Fuck!"

My hips stilled as I felt Jana's throat milking me as I came, moaning along with me. When she slowly backed away, kissing the tip of me, she collapsed against my thigh, panting as though I'd wrung one out of her when she'd pretty much sucked my brains out through my dick.

As my bearings returned, I bent to help her up to her feet, finding that telltale flush she only wore post-orgasm, and my eyes widened. "Goddamn, baby." I captured her lips with mine before I tilted her face up, so her eyes met mine. "Am I seeing things, or did you just come along with me?"

The apples of her cheeks pinkened further as she nodded. "Yeah."

"Hot damn, Jana. Come 'ere." I picked her up, carrying her to my bed as I lowered myself over her. "You up for another? I have yet to show you my appreciation for what you've just given me."

Lifting her arms above her head, her eyes met mine, her smile teasing. "Take me, Brycen. Do your worst. I'm all yours."

Jana

A text alert is what woke me the next morning, but instead of rushing to check my phone, I gingerly took the time to gauge how I felt.

My body ached in all the good places; my head lacked the headache I had expected after so much imbibing, and my stomach rumbled its need for sustenance with the subtle smell of caffeine in the air instead of an anticipated aversion to food.

Cracking one eyelid, I spotted a large glass of water and a small bottle of ibuprofen on the bedside table next to Brycen's alarm clock, along with a folded piece of paper.

Reaching for the note, I rolled onto my back and smiled at my man's messy script.

My man? I pondered over that idea, deciding I liked it—maybe even loved it.

Beautiful,

I left you some pain relief and water in case you need them this morning. Coffee is brewed. Come find me when you're ready for breakfast.

Love,

Brycen xxoo

Sitting up, I reached for the glass of water and chugged half of it before I got out of bed, leaving the pills aside, and stumbled straight for the en suite bathroom to take care of business.

Dressed in a pair of my favorite leggings and a loose sweat-shirt, I padded barefoot toward the kitchen, pouring myself a cup of coffee with the mug awaiting me on the counter, doctoring it the way I liked it, then held it with both hands, inhaling the sweet aroma before taking a sip.

Bailey's bark from the backyard had me looking toward the patio sliders, realizing the door was open.

A bare-chested, sweat-slicked Brycen graced me from the lawn as the man lay down, working on some sit-ups with the added difficulty of a medicine ball thingy he held against his chest.

Heat filled my cheeks and that horny bitch that was my pussy pulsed, despite last night's sexcapades. The man was *fine*.

Moseying off the patio, the coolness of the grass between my toes helped cool my raging libido as I approached him. I set my coffee down on the top step before getting closer.

"Morning, baby," Brycen said as he finished his rep, chucking the heavy ball to the side before he bent his knees, feet to the ground, and leaned onto one hand behind himself while extending the other to me.

Bending to him for a kiss, I smiled before saying, "Morning."

His eyes studied my face. "Feeling okay?"

On a self-deprecating laugh, I said, "Surprisingly, yeah. None the worse for wear."

He nodded. "Good. That means I can do this," he said, and in seconds, I found myself on the flat of my back, a smirking Brycen between my legs, before his mouth descended onto mine for an all-too-brief kiss. "Mmm." He nipped at my bottom lip before licking the sting. "You taste good. Hungry?"

Feathering my fingertips against the scruff on his face, I nodded. "Famished." Then I lifted my head to kiss him briefly again before, adding, "Now get off me, and feed me, mister."

It wasn't until Brycen went to put in a few hours in his office that I remembered my cell phone and the text alert I'd received. By the time I'd fetched the phone—which I'd left in Brycen's bedroom—the damn thing was dead.

Grabbing my Kindle and phone charger from the room I'd initially moved into—I still kept my things in there—I headed for the kitchen to plug it in, then made my way outside, Bailey dutifully following as I settled onto one of the lounge chairs warmed by the morning sun.

It was time to delve into Penny Sexton's upcoming release.

"Babe, sweetheart, wake up." Brycen's humored voice brought me back to the land of the living.

"Huh?" Taking in my surroundings, I realized I'd fallen asleep in the backyard, Bailey remained curled up at my side where I'd last spotted him.

"I promise I won't tell Aspen that you fell asleep while reading her book, but here." He handed me my phone. "It's been buzzing nonstop, and I figured you wouldn't want to miss anything if it has to do with your mom."

"Thanks." I leaned forward, cupping the back of his head, bringing his mouth to mine for a soft kiss.

"You stay here, check on those messages, and I'll make something quick for lunch." He kissed my forehead, then headed for the house.

twenty-six

BRYCEN

WHEN I'D CALLED Eloise this morning, I wasn't sure if she'd accept my mother's invitation to have her and Jana's brother join us for Sunday night dinner—but she had. Jason had decided to work, putting in some overtime, and so he'd begged off, citing that he'd join us for the next one.

"Are you sure it won't be too much for you, Mom?" Jana asked, turning toward the back seat of my car.

"Not at all." She winked at me when our gazes connected through the rearview mirror. "I'm just surprised it was Brycen who asked first."

I chuckled. "Seems your daughter had a little too much liquid fun last night. It wore her out so much she needed a midday siesta," I teased as I grabbed her hand, kissing her knuckle to soften the subtle jab.

"For that, I'm making your mother break out all of the baby pictures," she rebutted, and I groaned while Eloise simply giggled. I didn't really care in the grand scheme of things—I'd share all that I was with her if she let me, she just didn't know that factoid yet.

· · ·

As soon as we'd pulled up the drive, Mom was already out the front door, heading for my car before I'd helped Eloise out.

"Eloise?" Mom's eyes were rounded in surprise, reflecting recognition, but the upward tilt to her lips denoted that it was a welcome development.

"Helena?" Inspecting Eloise's expression, it became clear that both women knew each other from somewhere.

"Jeeze, Eloise, how long has it been?" Mom asked her before approaching her for a hug the other woman returned easily.

"It's got to be at least four by now. How's Pat?" Eloise asked.

"Still the love of my life." Mom laughed, grabbing on to Jana's mother's elbow, and started leading us toward the front door. "Just you wait until he sees who's come to dinner. What a small world."

Pulling Jana along with me as we followed our mothers into the house, I asked her, "Any clue how this happened?"

"Seeing as Mom used to be out more often than she was home before...you know, anything is possible." She studied the two women, her brows furrowing as her lips pinched. "It's weird. This feels weird. I'm not the only one who thinks it's weird, right?" she rambled.

"Oh, honey," Eloise interrupted us. "Let's sit down and we'll tell you all about the three of us."

"Mom!" Jana exclaimed, and our expressions must have been close to the same when both women burst out laughing, and Mom cupped the side of Jana's face tenderly before she lifted her other hand to cup mine.

"Oh hell, Brycen Matthews, I realize we're an open family that talks about pretty much everything, but it's not like that, so get that damn freaked-out look off of your face right now, mister." She patted at my cheek, then dropped her hands before she turned back to wrap her arm around Eloise's waist to escort her through the front door.

"Well, you did say *the three of us*, Mom," Jana stated, a deep blush spreading beyond simply her face.

"Sorry, ladies, but my mind went there too," I confessed.

"Well," Mom started, a teasing glint in her eyes as she turned to look at us over her shoulder.

"Mom!" I scolded. "I just can't. No! I don't want to hear about—"

"What in the world is going on out here?" Dad walked toward us from the living room, then came to a sudden halt. "Eloise?" he sputtered in disbelief.

"Pat," Eloise greeted, heading straight for his open arms, burrowing into his chest as if they were long lost family.

Again, Jana and I exchanged one of those *what the fuck* looks.

"Pat, I'd like for you to meet my daughter, Jana," she introduced.

"As in Brycen's Jana?" he said, peering over at me.

"That would be me," Jana laughed, her hand tightening around mine.

"Well hell," Dad said, releasing Eloise, who went straight to Mom's side, as my father reached for Jana's proffered hand, taking it only to pull her into his arms. "It's so good to finally meet you. Your mom's talked about nothing else but you and your brother over the years."

Years?

Jana

Turned out there was nothing untoward with how Brycen's parents and my mother had known each other. It shouldn't have surprised me that Mom would make friends in the most unlikely of places—least of all—one she'd volunteered at before she'd gotten sick.

"We miss your sassiness during our shifts." Helena leaned forward and grabbed on to my mother's hand. "Gourmet

Gateway hasn't been the same since you left us. You have to admit, it was all kind of sudden."

Mom's palm landed on top of the other woman's hand. "I'm sorry. I wasn't ready to talk about what was going on," Mom said, giving Helena's hand a squeeze as she looked at their joined hands. "It's been a rough go over the last four years." Her eyes met mine as she forced a smile. "And I'm afraid it might get bumpier before...before—"

"Mom." I grabbed her free hand. "You don't have to—"

A look of determination entered her eyes. "Oh, but I do, honey. We're amongst friends here, and as much as I've been hurting, it's time I make amends after hurting Pat and Helena."

"All is forgiven, E," Pat said softly. "We knew there'd have to be a good reason behind you going MIA so suddenly."

Mom nodded somberly, taking a deep breath before letting it all out. "I'm sick. It's cancer—breast to be more specific, and it's my second go at it."

A deep gasp escaped Pat while Helena threw herself at my mother. Brycen wrapped an arm around my shoulders, holding me tighter to him as I struggled to swallow the lump in my throat, staving off the tears that threatened to break the banks. Mom had never told a single soul except for our aunts and uncles, and even they knew so little of what was currently going on. This was a massive step for her. "Damn, Eloise, I'm so sorry."

"What can we do?" Brycen's father added as he leaned forward, supporting his wife with a hand on her shoulder.

"Whatever we can do is already being done," Mom explained, then sighed. "The kids have been wonderful, even though I'm taking up all of their extra time...and their space." Her shimmering eyes narrowed on me.

"You know that's not true, Mom," I argued. "I don't begrudge you and Jason living with me one bit, and you know he wouldn't have it any other way either, so get that out of your thick skull. We're family. We help each other out, and I wouldn't trade the time we've had together for anything in the world."

Mom turned to face me a bit more once Helena released her and cupped my cheek. "I love you, baby girl."

My vision blurred as I returned a, "I love you too, Mom," just as chaos ensued in the form of two little human tornadoes barging into the room.

"Uncle Bryce!" Two little terrors who looked almost identical and around the age of four came barreling down on us, pinning Brycen—and thus me—to the back of the couch.

"Hey guys!" He tickled first one, then the other, as both kids' bellowed delighted giggles. "I want you to meet someone." The boys paused to listen to the man at my side, eyes filled with worship. "This"—he edged his head toward me—"is Jana, my girlfriend." The boys' eyes went wide, and I swear my ovaries popped as soon as thrice the Matthews dimpled grins turned to face me.

"Hiya." I smiled at the two future heartthrobs.

"Tyson. Tyler. How many times do we have to tell you that we don't simply barge in on—" A short woman I'd never met before came to a halt in the living room's entry, an attractive man, with what I presumed was from native ancestry coming to a stop, towering above her and throwing a grin my way as he set his hands on the woman's shoulders.

"Mom," Tyler, or was it Tyson, said, as the other finished, "Uncle Bryce has a girlfriend!"

I couldn't help the giggle, nor could Brycen prevent the chuckle that came out when the second one who'd spoken made googly eyes and clutched at his chest on the word *girlfriend*.

Considering the resemblance between Brycen and this woman, this had to have been the remaining sister I'd yet to meet—Savannah.

"Savvy." Brycen scooted his sister's boys off his lap, got up, then held out his hand for me. "I'd like for you to meet—"

"Jana," she interrupted his introduction. "Did you honestly think I wouldn't know about the one who stole your heart, baby brother?" The woman stepped forward, stopping in front of me, then presented her hand. "I'm Savannah. Savvy to my friends and family. This big lug"—she nudged her head in the direction of the man at her back—"is my husband, Cooper. I'm so excited to meet you."

Giggling, I shook my head, then pulled her forward for a quick hug. "I know you're holding back and that y'all are huggers." Pulling away, I snuggled into Brycen's side. "It's nice to meet you both."

After dinner, I escaped to the bathroom, the excitement and din of a happy family feeling otherworldly and a tad overwhelming, if I was being honest. Between Brycen's sisters, there were five children and three husbands. I wasn't used to large family affairs unless it was a planned family reunion. Brycen's family was about the size of mine when we were all in the same room, but that hadn't happened in half a decade at this point.

Once my hands were dry, I chose to take a few extra minutes to check my phone, spotting a message from an anonymous source.

> UNKNOWN:
>
> There's nowhere you can go where I won't find you.

My stomach churned, my heart beat erratically, and I struggled to keep calm.

> I'll be seeing you soon.

"Fuck," I mumbled to the small powder room, peering into

the mirror in front of me as I braced myself and the ensuing dizziness threatening my equilibrium.

Just then, another message came through.

> It would be a shame if I had to destroy that beautiful family, but for you, I would. You took what was mine, which makes you mine, Jana. Mine.

And my worst fear was slowly becoming reality—leaving me with only one thing to do.

twenty-seven

BRYCEN

SOMETHING HAD BEEN NIGGLING at me since just after dinner at Mom and Dad's, but I couldn't quite pinpoint what it was, or when things had changed.

Jana had gotten progressively quiet and withdrawn as the evening wore on, and now that we'd just gotten back into the car after handing Eloise off over to Jason, who was back from work, I aimed to find out what was up with my woman.

"Everything okay?" I asked, threading my fingers through hers, giving her hand what I hoped was a reassuring squeeze.

"Huh?" She looked at me, then continued, "Oh, yeah. I'm okay. Just tired." Her smile looked a tad forced. "Your family is a lot, but I love them."

I smiled at that, lifting her hand so I could kiss her knuckles. "I still can't believe our parents knew each other."

She emitted a soft laugh. "Right?"

"Small world."

"Hmm," she agreed with a single nod. "I'm happy they got to reconnect."

Parking the car in the garage, I switched the vehicle off, then turned toward Jana, cupping the side of her face, glad when she nuzzled against my palm.

"Sweetheart?"

"Hmm?" She turned her head to kiss the side of my wrist, her eyes snagging mine.

Christ she was sweet. "Baby, you sure you're okay?"

Jana's hesitation was a moment too long for my liking and my gaze narrowed. "Come on," she said in answer, "I'm feeling just a little off-kilter after today, but I'm sure you can help me with that." She reached for the passenger side's door handle and started to exit the car, meeting me at the front of the hood after I exited.

As she grabbed on to the front of my shirt, I leaned closer, grabbing her face in my hands. "I'd do just about anything for you, baby, I hope you know that." I leaned in and kissed her forehead.

"Then take me to bed, Brycen," she whispered as I pulled back.

So that's what I did.

JANA

With one final look, I wiped the tears from my cheeks thanks to the too long sleeve of the sweatshirt I'd highjacked from Brycen's closet and closed the door behind me. Tiptoeing down the hall, I geared myself for a hasty retreat with nothing but the clothes on my back, a few more outfits in the backpack I'd pilfered from my borrowed bedroom, and my purse.

I loved him—Brycen Matthews.

But I couldn't stand by and risk his life...or his family's.

I couldn't risk Jason or Mom either, say nothing of the crew at Nightshade and their families who'd come to mean more than simple passing acquaintances.

Whoever this guy was, he'd shown me tonight he could get

to me no matter the magic mumbo-jumbo Devolin or Brycen could concoct with their computer genius minds.

It left me with no other choice but to run.

And that's what I was about to do.

A seedy motel on the outskirts of Jacksonville is where I decided to rest for the night—maybe the next couple of days, after having stopped at a random bank to withdraw as much money as the machines would allow me.

Once I was tucked away, locked tight in the mildew-scented room with a bed that looked as if something was growing within its mattress due to the lumpiness of it, I took my first breath, heading for the windows and closing the curtains.

Grabbing the rickety chair from the table in the corner, I added it as an extra layer of protection by wedging it under the room's door, double-checking the chain lock and deadbolt that looked as if it would snap off in my hand with little force.

Not for the first time, I questioned my sanity, let alone my decision on going at it alone.

Grabbing my purse, I dumped its contents on the tabletop, and started to remove the packaging from the two phones I'd picked up during my first stop after I'd fled Brycen and the safety of his arms. I knew that using the new cell phone Devolin had provided me a week and a half ago was a hard no, but I wanted to keep it on my person no matter what. I'd use it only if in dire emergency, but until such a time, I would leave the device charged up and turned off. Instead, I'd use the burners I'd procured, limiting my call times and alternating between devices so I wouldn't be traced.

Now what?

Now I waited.

Assessed my options.

And tried to bide my time until either this sicko was caught, or I found an alternative to disappear altogether—even if it killed me. I had the distinct feeling that things were coming to a head.

REX

"What the fuck?" I muttered in the emptiness of my truck, tucked away at the end of the row of motel rooms.

I was chasing a skip who was wanted for assault and battery of his girlfriend, and the woman's best friend, when I spotted an all-too-familiar woman cautiously peering over her shoulder as she unlocked the end unit closest to me.

Grabbing my phone, I dialed Matthews and as soon as the man answered, clearly having been asleep, I lit into him, "Where the fuck is your woman right now, Matthews?"

"Rex?"

"Yeah, Bryce, it's me," I growled, my blood at a low simmer. "Tell me your woman is snuggled up to you right now and I'm seeing things because I haven't slept for over forty-eight hours, chasing a skip. Tell me what I just saw less than fifty seconds ago was her doppelgänger, because, fucker, if Jana's who I saw at the No-Tell-Motel I'm scouting, heads are going to mother-fucking roll."

"Fuck," Brycen muttered under his breath, and I heard him scrambling across the line as the man evidently rushed to search his home if the slamming of doors was anything to go by, let alone the barking of his mutt. "Fuck! Fu-uck! She's gone, Rex."

A fire burned deep in my gut as I heard the bereft tone in the man's voice. "Fuck yeah, she is, but she ain't gonna be for long, Matthews."

"She'll be lucky if I ever let her up and out of bed before this shit is over and done with," Brycen grumbled. "Where you at?"

"Coastal, on Wilmington."

"Don't go in. I'm on my way." The man hung up before I could say anything else.

Flicking my phone onto the passenger seat, I tilted my head against the headrest and stared at my truck's ceiling. "Jesus, fuck! This is why I don't bother with women."

BRYCEN

Hitting up my office, I fired up the tracking program Devolin and I had built and tweaked. The partnered piece of this software had been installed on Jana's cell phone, a failsafe we'd snuck onto the device, thanks to too many close calls with past clients and some of NSI's women having upped and disappeared in the past.

When my cell buzzed, I hit *speaker* and growled, "No time, Huss."

"Too fucking bad, Babyface," she matched my growl in return. "You need to hear this. That fucker got to her. Just pulled up her message logs, and he's threatened those she loves most."

That's why she left? "When?" I demanded.

"Tonight. Uh, last night since it's just after three now."

Realization slammed into me right then. "Fuck."

Jana had behaved quieter than normal, withdrawn to the point of despondency. And when I'd pushed a second time to reassure myself that she was okay, thinking her state of mind had more to do about having spoken about her mom's declining health with my folks, and the exhaustion she claimed to be feeling, I couldn't have been further away from the truth.

"Can you turn on her phone?" I asked. "I'm on my way to her now, but I'm not waiting to talk to her. Forty minutes out is too fucking long for me to see for myself that she's safe, and I know she'd have turned off her phone before leaving here so she couldn't be traced. Rex just happened to be hunting a skip and he's sitting on her right now, so she's safe." *For now.*

"On it," Devolin confirmed. "Flicked the switch, and I'll let you know if anything changes. Bring her back, Bryce. She's one of us."

"You're fucking right she is, and it's high time she knows it too." Hanging up, I grabbed my phone, walked to the kitchen, and went for the weapon I kept stored in a secret compartment in a drawer next to the fridge, only to find it missing. Riffling through the compartment, the box of bullets I had there was lighter. Upon opening it, half of its contents were also missing.

Despite the terror that tried to choke me out, I ran to the safe in my bedroom closet, fetching the Glock I kept in there, checking that it was loaded, disengaging then reengaging the safety before tucking it into the back of my jeans, and grabbed the two loaded clips I kept beside it.

Bailey whined as I grabbed my keys, heading for the security alarm. "Sorry, boy, but it's time I go get our girl." Bailey barked then nudged at my pant leg. "Hold the fort for us." I gave him a reassuring scratch behind the ear.

After locking up, I rushed to my truck, opened the driver's side door, and cranked the ignition before I'd closed the door.

Shifting into gear, I dialed her number, hoping to holy hell I would be able to convince her to come home.

twenty-eight

JANA

THE MOMENT I heard my phone ping—and once I'd gotten over the confusion that the fucking thing was on again—I knew my night was about to go from bad to worse.

UNKNOWN:

> Kind of a dingy spot to be holed in, no?

The telltale bubbles of another text appeared, but my phone started a vibrating-ringing dance in my hands, that made me cry out in terror.

The comfort of seeing Brycen's name on my screen was short-lived, and I knew I couldn't ignore him.

Tapping the *Answer* button on the screen, I braced for what I would have to do next.

"Jana?"

His simple utterance of my name had me breaking down.

"Baby, don't hang up. Don't do this," he pleaded. "Please don't run."

I have to.

"You don't have to. We'll keep you safe, baby. We'll find him," his voice cracked.

"I can't risk losing you, Brycen, and that's what will happen if I stay," I explained, no longer caring about the tears that fell. "I-I can't—"

"Listen to me!" he growled down the line. "Devolin is working on tracing him. He knows where you are."

"I know!" I screeched. "It's why I have to go, Brycen. He'll kill again, and I can't have any of you at risk."

"Baby, we'll find him before he gets to you."

I shook my head. They wouldn't. Not before someone paid the ultimate price before then, and I'd be damned if I had to live with that guilt.

Just then, a text pinged, and I pulled the phone away from my ear to read it.

UNKNOWN:

I hope you're ready for me.

A shiver of dread washed through me, slithering down my spine. I had to get out of here.

"I love you, Brycen. Goodbye." Without another word, I hung up, powered down my phone, then walked to the bedside table, leaving it on its surface.

Grabbing my purse, I stuffed its former contents back into it, opened my backpack, and shoved it in there except for my car keys, which I deposited next to my phone.

Heading for the door, I turned every light off in the room, then moved the chair away from the knob, twisted the deadbolt to the unlocked position, and unsecured the chain. Erring on the side of caution, I hoped the cloak of darkness would help me make my getaway.

Noticing the same truck parked slightly around the corner from the room I'd rented, I was careful to move quickly in the event someone was in it. The feeling of being watched was unsettling, and I couldn't wait to get the hell out of Dodge.

When I reached the end of the row of rooms, I made my way for the trees lining the property's edge. If I followed the tree line long enough, I could stay close to the highway and maybe hitch a ride to the next town over.

I just hoped it would be enough.

BRYCEN

I love you, Brycen.

When I should have felt like I was on cloud nine as I heard those words for the first time, Jana's proclamation only gutted me.

I love you.

Goodbye.

"Like hell it's goodbye," I shouted to the interior of my truck.

As I pulled up to the dilapidated Coastal Motel, I slammed the brakes hard on my vehicle, coming to a stop next to what I knew was Jana's car. As soon as I spotted the front end of Rex's truck, fear filled me when I noticed the cab's interior lit up.

Making my exit, I kept an eye on my surroundings, withdrawing my Glock, and released the safety. I gripped it, ready to shoot anyone who came at me as I scaled the side of the building, using the wall as a shield in case someone lay in wait around the corner.

There's no way Rex would have left his vehicle for anything, and if he'd had to take care of business, he sure as shit would have never left his truck door open, let alone the cab light on.

Deeming the way clear, I turned the corner, and my blood ran cold.

On the ground, Rex lay unmoving, a growing pool of blood beneath him.

"Shit, Rex!" I analyzed my surroundings before scurrying to

my knees, feeling for a pulse and finding a very faint and thready one.

It took a bit to locate the source of his bleeding because the front of him was covered in the coppery fluid. Once I found the massive gash in his gut, I applied as much pressure as I could while I reached for my pocket to get my phone.

"Tell me she's with you," Dalton barked in answer.

"Negative." I took a breath and powered on. "Get Huss to dispatch an ambulance to the Coastal on Wilmington. Rex has been attacked."

"What?"

"Shit, D, it's not looking good," I announced, my voice cracking. "You've got to hurry. I'm putting my phone down because I've got to do something to help stop him from bleeding out. He was here—"

"Chasing someone down, yeah, Huss told me," the man gritted out. "I'm thanking the fucking Lord he was there long enough to ID your woman, but fuck, Bryce, this is getting messier by the day."

Tell me something I don't know.

"We're on our way." I heard voices in the background. "Ambo's out to you too. We're looking at about twenty. Keep him alive, Bryce."

"I'm trying." I spotted a sweatshirt on Rex's truck's armrest between the front seats, and scrambled to nab it, bunching the material up so I could use it as a compress to apply more pressure. "Just get here already." I pushed hard on Rex's abdomen, netting a groan, followed by a gurgle from my friend's throat.

The extended Nightshade gang congregated in Onslow Memorial's surgical waiting area, impatiently anticipating news on Rex's condition. The man had been brought in, having flatlined once in the back of the ambulance while I sat by and watched the medics work to bring him back. Thank fuck they had. I shuddered at the thought of how I'd deliver that news once we got Jana back had we lost him, and the reality was he still wasn't entirely in the clear.

Shortly after we'd arrived, the medics rolled Rex in while I headed to the nearest bathroom to wash as much of the man's blood off my hands as possible, changing into a set of scrubs an orderly brought me, but all I saw was red, and I was quickly losing my bearings.

I'd almost lost a good friend.

It looked as though I'd lost my woman—the love of my life—before we could really get our relationship off the ground.

And I had no idea if life as I had known it would ever be restored.

Two hours had passed since they'd wheeled Rex into surgery, and we'd yet to hear anything when Tate and Shane came striding into the waiting room.

Snapping to my feet, I rushed them, Shane putting his hands on my shoulders, a somber look on his face as Tate presented me with a Ziploc bag with what I recognized to be Jana's car keys—thanks to the hummingbird key chain—and the phone Devolin had given her.

"Truck's parked at NSI," Tate said as Shane told me what I already knew in my heart. "She's gone, man."

Reeling from his confirmation, I spun and punched the wall next to us, the drywall exploding once my fist met it. "Sonofabitch!" I roared.

A nurse came running, her eyes rounding with trepidation followed by her flaring temper. "Sir, I'm going to have to ask you to calm down or leave," the tall brunette said, her hands on her hips. "If you don't, I'll have to get security to escort you out."

Dalton waved her off as I let myself drop into the chair that was littered in dust and pieces of the wall I'd just smashed. "We've got this handled, Miss. He'll be good."

"You better," she griped.

"Here." He pulled out a business card from his pocket, presenting it to her between his index and middle fingers. "Please call us with an invoice for the damages."

With a curt nod, she snapped the card from his fingers, then turned to head back where she'd come from.

"What are we doing?" I rasped, running my hands down my face as I leaned forward on my knees. My brain had shut down and all I could do was worry about Jana—about Rex.

A small hand clasped my shoulder and I turned to find Devolin standing before me, tears streaming down her face while Dalton held her from behind. "We're going to find her, Bryce. I promise you."

"How? The only play we had was to activate her phone and hope she'd answer a text or a call," I told them all. "She left her fucking car so forget tracking her that way."

"She may have gone to ground, but you and Devolin are the best in the fucking business, Matthews," Tate stated, and I heard the agreeing murmur throughout the waiting area. "And don't forget, as soon as Rex is out of surgery and awake, he might have some information for us."

Another forty or so minutes went by before Rex's surgeon came looking for those awaiting news on Rex. The man had made it through surgery, but he was far from out of the woods, and would most likely have a lengthy recovery, and that was if he managed to avoid any secondary infections since one of his intestines had been nicked by the blade Tate and Shane had found at the scene.

CSI was still currently combing the motel's property to gather any and all evidence, and Shane, despite being a homicide detective, had taken it upon himself to keep the pulse on all matters pertaining to Rex's attack, as well as Jana's disappearance.

When a nurse made an appearance nearly two hours after we'd received the news that our friend and coworker had pulled through, she indicated only two of us would be able to see Rex now that he was awake.

"You guys are all family?" she asked as she led Dalton and me to his room.

"Something like that," D answered as we came to a stop by a room.

"You have five minutes," she said it as if she meant business. "The man was nearly eviscerated and needs to rest."

Dalton spoke for the both of us, but I nodded assent, "Got it."

Machines beeped, the smell of antiseptic was potent, and when Rex's eyes met mine, the defeated expression on his face had me hurrying to his side, even though he'd averted his gaze from mine by letting his head loll to the side away from me, on its pillow.

"Lost her, man," he whispered.

"Not your fault, Rex," I told him.

"Fucking asshole nearly gutted me," he added.

"I know. And damn am I glad he didn't succeed," I put a hand on and squeezed his shoulder nearest me.

"Wasn't the skip," he mumbled. "I've seen this fucker around though."

"Who?" Dalton pushed. "Rex, I don't want to rush you, but they've only given us five minutes."

"The prick who stabbed me." He swallowed hard. "Seen him before."

"You sure?" I asked, and Rex turned his head so his eyes met mine, and no matter the amount of drugs in his system, I knew he was lucid about his recollections.

"Get me a sketch pad, I'll fucking draw you a damn picture. Fucker's been lurking around everywhere."

I chuckled. "Buddy, you can't draw stick figures worth a damn." Looking up to Dalton, even he wore a smirk.

"For your woman, Matthews, you bet your ass I can." Rex closed his eyes and took a deep breath before he opened and met my gaze. "I fucking lost her," he repeated despondently.

"Rex, you couldn't help what happened," I told him.

Dalton cupped the man's other shoulder and squeezed gently. "And she's not lost. She went to ground. Now, it's up to us to put the pieces together and catch this psycho so she can come out of her hidey hole."

Rex grinned then. "He might have caught me by surprise, but I got a few licks in before I went down. There should be spatter on the rear driver's side fender. Man, I hope this fucker is in the system."

"I'll get Shane on it," Dalton said as his eyes met mine and he nodded toward the door.

"We'll let you rest. Be back in the morning, bud," I added.

"Hey, Bryce?" Rex croaked just as I was about to pass the room's threshold.

I turned to face him. "Yeah?"

"Give her hell when you find her, will ya?" The man gave me a pained smile.

"Tell you what," I returned, feeling my lips tug upward in my first real smile since I'd woken up without Jana. "When I get her back, I'll fucking make sure she knows how I feel, and then I'll redden her ass so much she won't be able to sit comfortably for a week."

And I meant every goddamn word, and maybe a few more I simply wasn't about to share, because Jana deserved to hear those words first.

twenty-nine

JANA

IT HAD BEEN three days since I'd last seen or heard from anyone, and the four walls of the hellhole I currently called my refuge were starting to close in on me.

I'd killed a total of ten creepy crawlies every day since my arrival, and don't get me started on the rustling between the walls I keep hearing at all hours of the day—*and* night. Suffice to say, I was disgusted, a little terrified with what Mother Nature was going to dish up for me next, but I was fed, I was warm, and most of all, I was safe.

But I was alone.

Sure, I had my Kindle, but that sucker had run out of power this morning, and this hunting shack I'd stumbled upon on my attempt to get out of town had no power source. Believe me, I'd looked. And forget about books or old magazines for entertainment. Never mind a generator or even running water—I was lucky I'd found a hand-pump well and a semi-decently clean, albeit dusty bucket to fill so I could stay hydrated and clean up after myself.

As I washed my lunch dishes, consisting of a fork, because

I'd eaten beans directly from a can I'd heated up with the help of a small fire. Said fire had been promptly put out once I'd finished cooking. I wasn't taking any chances that someone discovered my location.

Despite my unorthodox safe haven, dread and worry had grown in the pit of my stomach over the course of time. Call it a sixth sense, but I felt the sudden urge to call home, to check on Mom and Jason.

I still had those two burner phones on me and was currently looking at one of them on the edge of the tiny table I had just deposited my cleaned fork on.

"You'd be lucky if you have reception," I snorted at the ridiculousness of my reality. "Great. Now look at you…talking to yourself." I shook my head as I dried my hands on the raggedy hand towel next to the small bowl I was using as a sink and had an epiphany.

As much as this little cabin in the woods had served as a very humble refuge, my favorite part about it was the Adirondack chair that sat on the decrepit covered porch.

Fed and bored out of my skull with nothing but worry for those I loved, I leaned forward and pondered the phone in my hand. A conversation I'd had with Devolin a few weeks prior had come back to me. It had been something about a client who'd relied on her original cell phone's voicemail to communicate that she was safe. By using a burner, and minimizing the amount of time she spent on it, she had been virtually undetectable, but able to utilize her personal voicemail to leave breadcrumbs to be saved.

A tiny ember of hope took root, and for the first time since that Sunday dinner, I wanted to reach out to my people instead of run from them—just to let them know I was safe.

What I hadn't expected was the fifty-four messages that

greeted me when I'd punched in the pin to my old phone number.

The first three had been old messages I'd saved, regarding a variety of appointments for Mom.

The next was from Devolin, explaining she understood why I'd left, but that no one blamed me for what happened to Rex. She went on to tell me he'd been at the motel that night, been attacked, but he pulled through surgery, and he should make a full recovery. Next, she went as far as to let me know I was stupid if I thought she and Brycen would fail at finding me. She closed with letting me know everyone was worried but hoped I was somewhere safe, and they were doing everything they could to locate my stalker.

Now, more than ever, the news about Rex served to prove that I'd made the right decision to disappear and stay away until everything was resolved.

The next few messages had come from work, asking for a report on how I was doing, wondering when I might end my leave and come back to work.

"What part of being stalked by a serial killer does Steven Saxon not understand?" I asked aloud, the wind in the treetops doing nothing but mocking me in its whispering ways.

The following five messages were delayed hang-ups, where I could barely hear shallow breathing on the other end—something reminiscent of when this psycho first fixated on me—and it gave me the willies. But I saved them until such a time Dev or Brycen was able to analyze them if they hadn't begun the task already.

The next dozen or so calls were from Mom and Jason, all of them denoting their worry for my safety, ensuring that I knew they loved and missed me, and begging me to come home.

When the next message came on, my breath hitched at the vulnerability in Brycen's voice.

"Jana, baby...By the time you get this, I hope to God that I finally have you in my arms again. But if by some miracle, you've figured

out how to get to your voicemail, I need you to know I love you," he sighed. *"Sweetheart, I love you so goddamn much. You've been gone for less than twenty-four hours, and the worry is tearing me up inside. Please come home. I love you."*

It had taken me nearly an hour to get through all the messages, simply because I had listened to some of them a few times over before saving them so I could listen to them again later, and then I took a chance and prayed it didn't blow up in my face.

BRYCEN

Four days went by without a word or sign of life, and then the alarm on my computer went off about the same time my cell phone chimed with the alert signaling there was activity on Jana's phone.

Stumbling from the couch in my office, tripping over the assortment of discarded takeout containers and two fifths of Jack I'd killed off that had littered my office floor since Jana had disappeared, I hit the *enter* key on my keyboard to silence the incessant beeping, and went to work, not quite believing what I was seeing.

Had our messages finally worked?

My cell rang with Devolin's ringtone, and I was quick to answer, "You're seeing this, right?" I croaked in way of a greeting.

"I wouldn't be calling if I wasn't."

"Any news on the labs?" I asked about the DNA located at the scene of Rex's attack.

"Perp is Carson Platt," she answered on a snort. "I'm still looking into him and what ties he may have to Jana, and it'll take me a while because there's a lot there, but I'll get what I need, don't worry, Bryce. I'm sending you what I've gotten so far. You should get it before we hang up."

Realizing she couldn't see my nod, I said, "'K, thanks." I gave a quick glance at what Devolin sent over, then asked, "Got it. Do we have a bead on him at least?"

The woman groaned. "Shane said they stopped by his home. No one's there, but they've put a couple of units on his place of residence and work. If he shows, we'll get him."

"I want to know as soon as anyone gets anything, Huss," I growled. "I need her home."

Devolin sighed. "I know you do. We all do. Now, Kip is on his way into the office, and as much as I know you don't want to leave the house, I'm not patching you in this time. Do what you have to, check up on the latest off our girl's phone, then get here."

Before I could argue, she'd hung up.

I'm safe. I'm close. I-I'm sorry about what happened to Rex. I thought that if I'd left... she sighed. *I'll touch base soon.*

It's all Jana had left us over her voicemail, but it went a long way to assuage my worst fear, which was of her lying in some ditch or dumpster somewhere after this Platt character had managed to get his hands on her.

The moment I set foot in the war room, everyone turned to face me.

"Shit, Bryce, you look like the walking dead," Theo stated the obvious, albeit with a sympathetic expression. He knew what I was going through, and if I'd taken the time to breathe through the melee of emotions running through me, I'd have remembered that most of us in this room had been through something similar in recent years.

"Have you slept at all?" Tate added with a sympathetic expression, the question filled with hesitant concern more than his typical tongue-in-cheek tone.

"Talk to me about sleeping when you find the love of your fucking life and she goes missing," I barked, letting myself drop in one of the few remaining conference room chairs, then crossed my arms over my chest. "Can we please get on with anything new so I can go back to—"

Devolin came rushing into the room, a shit-eating grin on her face. "We've got him. JPD received a number of tips where he's been spotted near Onslow Memorial. One of our sources spoke to him. She called it in as soon as she saw his picture on the news."

Dalton's body went rigid as did the rest of ours, concern for our friend and colleague. "Our guy is still on Rex?" he demanded.

Huss confirmed with a single nod, her body vibrating with excited energy. "Called him before rushing in here. All is quiet and he hasn't seen the perp. He's sticking close in case it's why Platt is there to begin with."

"Right," Dalton met all our gazes one by one, settling on mine last with a note of determination. "I'm not stopping you from tagging along, but you're taking a back seat on this one, Matthews. I want everything by the book until Platt's in custody, got me?"

I tilted my chin up in agreement. "Got you, boss."

The man gave me a curt nod. "Good."

"Let's roll out," Cade called to our group.

Jana

An hour ago, when I received an encrypted text from Brycen, on an app he'd requested I download through a voicemail he'd left on my original number, it said the NSI team had a suspect thanks to Rex recognizing his attacker's face—thank God he was okay. Hope bloomed that this whole nightmare would soon be over. The message contained a link to a local news site that had posted his name and picture.

Morbid curiosity urged me to take a look and so I clicked on it—a microscopic image of a man's face I couldn't recall popped up, reality hitting me square in the face.

Sure, having a name and a face might help the FBI and local authorities with their case, but it sure as shit didn't do anything for me.

And then I used that same encryption messaging app to message my brother with the information, again, reiterating I was somewhere safe, that I loved them.

When his response came in, however, informing me Mom had been hospitalized, I panicked.

Thus, it was why I had hitched a ride, thanks to an older lady who'd taken pity on me, then dropped me off at a small gas station at the edge of Jacksonville's city center.

After having used the facilities to clean myself up, I asked the clerk behind the counter if I could use their landline. Hanging up the phone after having called a taxi, a shudder ran through me when I saw that all-too-haunting face appear on the TV mounted on the wall behind the cashier's counter.

"Ma'am, you okay?"

My eyes strayed from the television to the woman behind the counter, catching a glimpse of the pale reflection mocking me from one of the drink cooler doors.

"Uh, y-yeah. Yes." I gave the lady a curt nod, noticing the cab I'd ordered had pulled up. Hurrying toward the station's door, I turned and forced a smile. "Thanks again for letting me use your phone."

"Don't mention it." The lady studied me from head to toe, and I had a sneaking suspicion she saw more than I wanted her to right then. "Stay safe, you hear?"

Clearing my throat, I nodded once more. "Will do." I made my retreat, attempting to steel my nerves.

"Where to?" the middle-aged man who sounded like he'd adopted a pack-a-day habit since birth rasped.

"Onslow Memorial Hospital, please." Refusing to meet his gaze in the rearview mirror, I buckled up and kept watch on the passing scenery.

A chirp from my back pocket had me reaching for the burner I'd stuffed in my jeans so I could easily access it, finding another text from my brother.

JAY:

Where the fuck are you?

Chewing on my thumbnail, I pondered if I should respond or merely show up? I felt more comfortable with no one knowing my whereabouts, but this was my brother.

I'm on my way. Tell Mom I love her. Love you.

Jason then texted back with the room number.

It took the cab forty minutes to get to Onslow, and I paid the driver with some of the cash I had withdrawn when I first set out to disappear.

Knowing this place like the back of my hand from having worked a mere four years here as a nurse, before calling it quits due to too many losses, it wasn't too hard to navigate through the throngs of people and families in the emergency department.

Taking a quick glance around, I snuck into the stairwell entry, and headed for the fifth floor meant for admitted patients.

Hoofing it up to the fifth had me huffing and puffing, swearing to myself that once this was all over, I'd revisit the idea of making use of my local gym's Stairmaster. I haven't felt this out of shape since my first week here as a nurse.

Collecting myself, I took a deep breath and pulled on the door, giving a cursory glance at both ends of the halls. Heading to the left, according to the directional signs indicating which rooms were located down which hall, I attempted to shake off the ever-present sensation that someone was watching me.

Just as I turned to peer over my shoulder, a hand covered my mouth and nose, and I was violently pulled back into a dark room, held against a solid chest.

"Ah-ah-ah," the clearly male voice chided me at the same time I felt the coolness of something sharp near my jugular, paralyzing me with terror. "We wouldn't want to ruin this moment, would we?" He removed the hand that covered my mouth, circling it around my stomach.

"P-platt," I stutter-whispered, attempting to figure out where we were. I couldn't see much of anything for fear of his blade slicing into my neck if I turned my head, so I stood still.

His breath was warm at the side of my face, vile smelling, and when he rubbed his cheek against mine, pressing his torso into my ass, my stomach nearly revolted then and there.

"Got it in one go, sweetheart," he chuckled lowly. "Now, be a good girl and maybe I won't kill you like I did the others."

thirty

Brycen

"GOT HIM!" Devolin exploded through the silence of the hospital's security room where she and I had set up shop with the two security officers on shift. "He's still on the grounds," she relayed to our team through our earpieces.

A slew of copies came through loud and clear from the team as Shane came back with "Inside or out?"

"Still scouring the footage to confirm," I said, then shifted to the cameras covering the areas with public entrances we'd just sighted Platt in.

"There!" Devolin pointed to the fourth monitor from my left. "South entrance. What's the door number or entrance name?" she demanded from the officers.

"It's the main entrance to our education center," one of them answered.

Nodding at the man, I clicked my comms unit so I could relay the information to the rest of our team. "South side, left of main entrance off of Western Boulevard. Education Center."

Acknowledgement followed as the four of us continued to trace Platt's steps.

"Isolate the interior footage nearest and around the education center," I directed. Within seconds, the system refreshed with ten alternating views of the center and the areas that led to the hospital's main entrance and the adjoining cafeteria area.

It took some navigating, but we'd managed to follow him up to the fifth floor.

"Pull up a list of patients admitted to that floor," Devolin demanded one of the officers, the one who was merely tagging along.

"That's confidential," he argued.

"And you've got a serial killer in here, along with the local JPD, NSI, and the fucking FBI, now get me that fucking list," she demanded again.

It took him thirty seconds to pull the thing up and nearly a minute of syncing that list with all of Carson Platt's known contacts—and we got nothing.

"Run his name against any patients admitted in the last ten years, Huss," I instructed as my phone pinged. Pulling it out, I found a new alert from Jana's phone, along with a few I'd missed that were a few minutes apart. "Fu-uck!"

Devolin's eyes assessed me for a split second before returning to her laptop's screen. "What?"

"Jana's on her way here. Looks like she's been texting Jason, but I don't recognize the number," I told her, punching the digits into my reverse lookup tool.

"Shit," Devolin muttered. "How much you willing to bet that asshole spoofed her brother's phone again?"

Exactly what I'm thinking, Huss.

When my alert system notified me Jana had arrived at the hospital, I hightailed it from the basement security quarters to intercept her.

After verifying Jason and Eloise were both home and neither had attempted to contact Jana within the last twenty-four hours, the authorities and NSI team knew Jana had been lured out of hiding with the guise Platt had established. Knowing my woman as I did, it was a foolproof stunt—the ever-dutiful daughter that she was, and the impending loss of the only parent she had—was a perfect ploy.

Devolin came through my earpiece as I spun around in slow circles, taking in the main entrance's areas, moving around to make sure I got a proper visual of all the nooks and crannies between there and the cafeteria, and the elevator banks. "North side of the elevators, Bryce. She took the stairwell about two minutes ago."

"Copy."

Sprinting in that direction, I blasted through the doors, pausing to listen, but it was useless. Other than the pounding of my heart in my ears, I couldn't hear anyone else's footsteps.

"Anyone up on the fifth?"

"Theo and Cade are up there," Dalton cut in. "Got an agent and a few JPD officers starting on a room-by-room search right now."

"She's gone left of the stairwell, Bryce," Devolin said.

"Got it," I growled, making a mad dash up the stairs as fast as my feet could carry me.

JANA

My body shook from the buildup of adrenaline in my bloodstream, and I couldn't seem to process my thoughts adequately.

"W-why are you doing this?" my teeth chattered as I spoke.

The chest at my back rumbled with Platt's muted amusement. "You mean you and your merry band of men haven't figured it out yet?"

"N-no," I pushed myself closer to him in an effort to get away from his knife.

In a swift move, Carson Platt had me backed against the door to what now—after my eyes had adjusted to the lack of lighting—I could make out to be a janitorial closet.

Instead of the blade he still brandished, his forearm pressed against my windpipe, and I struggled to get air to breathe as spots floated around my vision's periphery due to both lack of oxygen, but also the way my head had smacked against the door.

"You used to be a nurse." Spittle hit my face. "How is it that you can play God and I can't?" He pushed harder against my throat, causing me to gag. "It took me four tries, but when you gave my victims your name, and when I heard that oh so sympathetic voice of yours, I'd recognize anywhere, I knew I had you."

My hands came up, clawing at his forearm, but when that didn't work, I tried to turn my head to the side to see if the pressure on my neck would ease off. It didn't, so I pushed up onto my tiptoes—the suspicion of where we'd crossed paths irrelevant for the moment.

"I've never play-played G-god," I choked out.

He sneered as he said, "Oh, but I beg to differ, sweetheart. My *wife* would beg to differ as well. I'll have to enlighten you when we get to where we're going."

The crassness with which he said *sweetheart* grated on me, and my blood simmered with rage.

No one calls me that but Brycen, no one!

Platt put a stop to my rising knee by releasing my throat and spinning me around, slamming my face into the door, then pressing my cheek into it. Blackness infringed on my vision, and the sticky trickling of warmth told me my nose was bleeding—possibly broken.

"I hate to ruin our reunion," he rasped, slapping a hat onto his head, the bill nudging my temple, "but it's time we get gone. Thanks to the muscle at the motel, the authorities know who I am. It's only a matter of time before someone's on our tail."

"Like hell." I licked my dry lips, tasting the coppery flavor of my own blood, letting out an unamused laugh, saying the next with more conviction. "Like hell you will. Even if I were to cooperate, you said so yourself, your face is all over the local news. How do you plan to justify the blood on my face, huh?"

TATE

"Anyone check the supply and janitors' closets?" Cade asked when we'd completed the sweep of the patient rooms. "Huss confirmed Jana's up here on this floor, same as Platt, and yet, no one's seen them?" The man snorted his disgust that we'd come up short, while I tried to keep my mounting frustration internalized because Matthews was about to join us.

"The head nurse is getting the access card now," the FBI special agent answered. "I made the request while I waited for you guys to finish up."

Before we got started, a muffled thump came from a closed door that boasted the image of a mop and bucket on the wall next to it.

Nodding to the group of men to follow me, I approached, careful not to bring attention as I heard a few of them rustling, most likely doing what I was, which was drawing my service weapon in case trouble came of this.

Holding a finger to my lips for silence, I pressed my back against the wall, and leaned my head closer to see if I could detect anyone.

As a second, much louder thump came against the door, I looked to my feet and shook my head on a "Shit," escaping me.

"What is it?" Cade asked in a hushed tone.

"You're going to want to clear this entire section of the floor, right the fuck now," I whisper-barked. "They're in there, and I think she's hurt."

thirty-one

BRYCEN

"MATTHEWS, WE'VE GOT THEM," Tate said through the comms as I was just arriving to the fifth floor.

"Thank fuck," I breathed, then asked the burning question. "Is she okay?"

"She sounds hurt, but we haven't gotten to them yet. Thought we'd wait on you to streamline our approach, but I suspect we ought to hurry because I think he's about to try and get away with her," my coworker announced.

"Like hell," I growled. *Over my dead body.* Rushing from the exit to the stairwell, I spotted Tate and Cade, heads bent close at the nurses' station. "Where are the others?"

"Minimizing the chance for casualty and injury," Cade said, gripping his weapon in his right hand. "Should be good to go any minute now since everyone is mobile."

On a singular nod, I spotted a JPD officer approaching. "Brycen Matthews, good to see you, despite the circumstances," James, a JPD officer I'd worked with in the past, offered up his hand which I shook.

"Thanks for the assist," my voice rumbled out.

210

"

"Should be thanking you," he smirked. "We doing this?"

"Fuck yeah," Cade and I said over one another.

In minutes, things unfolded rather rapidly.

First, Tate grabbed the keycard while the lone FBI agent, who had accompanied James and his partner, stood in a semi-circle along with Cade and me, weapons at the ready, on point for any advantageous angle. As soon as my coworker made it to the door, he grabbed the handle with one hand, using the barrier as a shield as he swiped the card.

The moment the door flew open, Jana flew back, the momentum propelling her to the floor, leaving a stunned Carson Platt sprawled overtop of her, his hand brandishing a large military pocket blade still at her neck.

Panic hit me when I saw the blood, unsure if Jana had been cut, or if what I saw was from the broken nose I unmistakably detected.

"Drop the knife and put your hands up, Platt." James approached slowly, his gun aimed to do more than maim if he had to.

Instead of listening, Platt sat up, straddling Jana's torso, holding her down by the throat with his free hand as his gaze met mine. The sickening grin on the man's face made me want to wretch, while the gurgling coming from Jana's throat as she struggled for breath, scrambling and clawing at the man's arms, gave me the urge to kill.

In seconds, Platt reared the arm that held his blade and as his arm arced downward, gunpowder and lead was released multiple times, the final percussions of the shots followed by the metallic clanging of the now unmanned weapon.

Jana

"Jana." The voice sounded muffled. "Jana, can you hear me?"

As my faculties returned, everything hurt. But I could breathe again. I must have blacked out because when my eyes opened, I was swimming in chocolate pools.

"Let me check her out," a familiar voice said. "Back up," she demanded in that habitual no-nonsense tone of hers. "I swear, you men will be the death of me one of these days. Fucking soldier boys," Dr. Reina Boudreaux grumbled.

"N-no," my voice cracked, my vocal cords feeling like they hadn't been used for months, probably due to all the choking I'd endured.

"Don't speak, Jana," Dr. Boudreaux ordered with that Louisiana twang of hers.

Meeting her eyes, I did the exact opposite to her instruction. "Brycen stays…please." Tears escaped the sides of my eyes as soon as I felt his hand clutching mine.

"Right here, baby," he rasped, and the emotion in those words only made me cry more.

"Jana, I'm going to check those wounds out and determine if you need a C-collar so we can move you to a gurney, all right?" Reina clutched my other hand and shook her head, gracing me with that crooked smirk of hers. "Christ, Jana, I didn't think the next time I saw you was going to be like this."

Mouthing "Sorry," my lips pressed into a hard line as she began to palpate around my neck, the back of my head, then checked for signs of a concussion.

"Your tracking is good, and your faculties seem to be all there," she murmured, then met my eyes. "Any dizziness, nausea, or headache? There's a slight lump at the back of your head and, honey, your nose is going to have to be set."

"Head…ache," I broke up the words.

"Okay," Reina whispered, squeezing my hand. "We're going to move you to a chair and wheel you to a bed. It's pointless to send you down to Emergency at this point since I'm keeping you overnight. I'll get Vanessa to come clean you up in a bit, and when she's done, I'll be back to set your nose."

"Urgh," I mumbled, causing the woman to laugh. "You're going to enjoy that, aren't you?"

Reina grinned, then winked. "It'll be payback for the time you had to set my broken finger after I slammed that fucking car door on it."

"Right." I shook my head, then looked to Brycen, my gaze captured by his. "He stays."

His eyes darkened, and his hand squeezed mine again. "Not going anywhere without you, sweetheart. Never again," he promised.

After retching from the pain of having my nose set—sans Brycen for that less-than-delightful experience—whatever painkiller I'd been given had knocked me out cold. I'm sure the lack of sleep I'd had since running away had also been a contributing factor.

"There she is," Brycen whispered into my ear as I groggily awoke.

"Hey," I drawled, smiling as our eyes connected and I squeezed the hand he still held clasped around mine.

"Hey, baby." He got up from his bedside chair, leaned forward and pressed his lips gently to mine before pulling away to study me, sitting on the edge of my hospital bed. "How are you feeling?"

"My face feels like I went twelve rounds with Mike Tyson, but I'll live." I shrugged my shoulders, his eyes darkening in a menacing way.

"Please don't crack jokes about what we've just gone through." He rested his forehead against my shoulder, and I clasped the back of his neck with my free hand.

The scruff of his cheek rubbed against mine, and I couldn't help myself, allowing my fingertips to play with it as he pulled away, an amused gleam in his eyes, despite the seriousness of the moment. "I missed this scruff." Leaning up, I kissed his cheek. "I missed you, Brycen." Then my lips met his other cheek before I pulled away once more to gaze into his eyes. "I missed us," I whispered against his lips, then finished with what I'd been aching to tell him face-to-face since the day I ran. "I love you."

"I love you too, Jana," he rasped against my lips, his heart in his eyes, and then he sealed our joint declaration with a soul-searing kiss—one that felt as though it had gone on for an eternity, yet still wasn't long enough.

None of that mattered, however, because if I had any say in things, I planned to ensure Brycen Matthews was my forever.

thirty-two

IT WAS late morning the day after we'd taken down Carson Platt by the time Jana was able to breathe freely. The day had started with a visit from Eloise and Jason, followed by one from the FBI. JPD came in after the FBI had left, and there'd been little time for a break between interviews.

After an in-depth update on what Devolin had been able to turn up on Platt, we'd finally been able to put the pieces of the man's obsession over Jana together. Carson Platt had held Jana responsible for the death of his wife, a little over seven years ago, when she'd been a nurse at Onslow Memorial. With Platt's wife's patient file at her fingertips, Devolin was able to confirm Jana had been her nurse the night the woman had been brought into the ER, but she'd also established Jana had never been part of the reason behind the woman's loss of life. The woman's file had stated suspected domestic abuse, but somehow, the hospital had failed to report their suspicions. Additionally, Platt had been so disturbed with the loss of his wife, he'd ended up being treated for an acute anxiety episode.

Jana explained she had left her job as a nurse around that

same time, due to having a hard time coping with patient loss and the high demands that came with treating the next patient, with little to no support from the hospital when their employees needed it for their mental well-being. She wanted to be able to help those in need on some of the worst days of their lives, but she no longer wanted to be in the action. Her job as a dispatcher had given her that, and the supports from the city were amazing and readily available.

With Platt being dead, there was no way to confirm the reason behind the man's murders, but when looking closer at the three victim's photos, Aspen had been the one to point out the women's resemblances to Jana. With that in mind, Shane and James from the JPD hypothesized the three women had been victims of opportunity by simply having crossed Platt's path. He'd killed them with no regard as to who they were, the marks on their bodies embodying the rage within him.

Now that things had settled, I'd managed to answer a few of Jana's lingering questions, the latest pertaining to how Rex was doing. And thus, it was why I was escorting her to see the man himself.

"Oh, my God!" she gasped as soon as we walked through the threshold to Rex's room.

Rex turned his head to face the doorway and glared at my woman. His outstretched arm was a contradiction, but I understood Jana's hesitation in finishing her approach.

"Get over here, woman," his voice cracked.

Standing behind Jana, I put my hands on her shoulders the moment she took a hesitating step back. "It's okay," I reassured her, kissing the crown of her head.

Her feet hesitantly brought her forward and judging by the softness in Rex's expression—not to mention the glossiness in his eyes—Jana was shedding silent tears for the bear of a man.

"This is-this is m-my fault," she hiccupped, brushing the

sleeve of the sweatshirt over her cheeks. Devolin and Dalton had brought a set of pajamas and some clothes for today so she would have something comfortable to lounge in until she was discharged this afternoon.

As soon as Jana was close enough, Rex latched on to her wrist and pulled her to the side of his bed, clutching her hands in his massive ones. "Now, I know you're trying to shoulder all of the blame, but you know as well as I do that you're full of shit on that one, Janice Elway."

"I-it's Jana." Her words came out sounding half-hiccupped, half-growled.

Smirking, Rex continued, "I was the unlucky sonofabitch to be there at the wrong time...or maybe it was the right time because, if I wasn't there chasing that skip of mine, I'd have never known where you were, nor would I have picked up on that Platt twat. If he hadn't stabbed me, I wouldn't have fought, and that man's DNA—the only piece of him that pointed to him —would have never landed on my back fender."

"B-but—"

Stepping forward, I wrapped my arms around her torso, letting her lean into me. "No, baby." My voice cracked. "If you're looking for someone to blame for the bad stuff, that shit all lies on Carson Platt. Rex knows it, I know it, you know it, and the whole damn state of North Carolina probably knows it by now."

"O-okay," she whispered, wiping at her damp cheeks once more, "but I reserve the right to beat myself up over having left and caused panic."

Tilting her chin up to the side as I leaned over her shoulder, our eyes met, and I put as much conviction into my voice. "And we'll be talking about that in due time, sweetheart."

"Should have heard this guy when I first came out of surgery." Rex smirked. "Brace yourself, Jana, because that man right there, he's got an itchy palm."

Jana turned to face me, her face colored with a delightful blush I hadn't seen in far too long. "Itchy palm?" She seemed to fight the urge to laugh or appear appalled, but settled somewhere in between when she asked, "Do I want to know?"

Cupping the side of her face, I grinned down at her. "Oh, trust me, baby, you'll find out soon enough what an itchy palm feels like."

With that, Rex's explosive laugh resonated throughout his room before it came to a screeching halt with a loud hiss. "Oh, oh, fuck." He took a deep breath. "Shit." Another. "Laughing hurts." And another. "Duly noted."

At that, both Jana and I dissolved into laughter, the heaviness of the moment lifting, and for the first time since I'd laid eyes on my love again, I knew that all would be okay.

Jana

The sound of a throat clearing behind us had me spinning so fast Brycen had to grab the sides of my arms to prevent me from toppling over.

"Thought I'd find you in here once the uniforms finally cleared out," Reina smirked. The expression dissipated the moment her eyes strayed to Rex however, and I wondered what that was all about, considering Rex was grinning wide.

"Well, well, we meet again, Doc." Rex's words were syrupy. "Missed me already?"

Brycen harrumphed, and I tried and failed to cover up the giggle that inadvertently seeped out through the hand covering my mouth.

"Hardly," she muttered with an eye roll.

"I think you might want to check his stitches, Doc." Brycen's voice held certain humor, and I caught the wink he threw Rex while Reina wasn't looking. "The guy busted a gut just a few short minutes ago."

"I'm sure his stitches are fine," my former coworker answered nonplussed, yet fought that upward tick of her lips like the woman of steel I'd known her to be. She waved a few pages in my direction. "Got your discharge papers here. Thought you'd want to go home and find some normalcy again. How's your nose?"

"With the degree of pain you inflicted on it yesterday, it's either going to heal looking better than before, or you'll be paying for plastics to fix it once the swelling goes down," I joked, Reina's eyes lighting up with matching humor.

"Tit for tat, right?" she singsonged.

"Right," I muttered, then held out my hand for the papers. "Let me see those. I can't wait to put this shitstorm behind me."

"By the way, I'm kind of pissed at you right now." Reina crossed her arms over her chest, her gaze probing. "I know I skipped out on you for drinks four weeks ago, but shit, Jana, what the hell? A man? A stalking serial killer?" Her eyes were wide with disbelief. "Again, I say, What. The. Hell."

"Feels like a lifetime ago instead of a month," I mumbled as I signed on the few lines, checking a few boxes along the way before handing the papers back to her. "Everything happened so damn fast." I paused to look at the man who sat in the chair next to Rex's bed, the two having watched the entire exchange with much curiosity. Brycen's eyes were filled with devotion and protection, while Rex's gaze was one closer to infatuated interest. I couldn't blame him, really, my girl was hot. Shaking the thought out of my head, I grinned at the man I had finally taken a chance on.

"Jesus." My gaze snapped back to Reina. "Never thought I'd see the day this girl fell. Love looks good on you, girl. And with that, I've got to get going. My shift's about to end and I can hear my bed calling me."

I swear I heard Rex mutter, "You sure it ain't my bed calling you?" under his breath, but either Reina hadn't heard him, or she chose to ignore him.

With a quick hug, Dr. Boudreaux took her leave, and while I headed straight for Brycen's lap, my eyes busied themselves with assessing Rex, trying to figure the man out, unsure if I'd ever get that man pegged.

REX

As my eyes followed *the* Dr. Reina Boudreaux, I felt two sets of questioning gazes burning into the side of my face—so I did what any self-respecting manly asshole would do—I stalled.

Beating the pillow at my head into some state of submission, I leaned back and closed my eyes, feeling Brycen and Jana's still on me.

Jana was the first to break. "Okay, spill, dude," she huffed.

"Met her last year when Cade and Aspen had their thing," I explained. "Don't know her past that." I wasn't going to go into how I'd known *of* her, however.

"Uh...huh," was what came out of Jana, Brycen chuckling at her back.

"Anyway," I grumped but turned to look at the happy couple, glad they had found what they had, just like the others, even though it wasn't for me. "Aren't you two on your way home now?"

Brycen's knowing smirk faded to a look of determination as he gave me the chin lift, a universal signal between us NSI guys that meant he got me. "Right." Then he tapped Jana's hip, helping her to her feet. "Let's get you home and into our bed, baby. I'm fucking wiped, and you need to rest."

Jana's eyes narrowed on Brycen but the subtle lift to the edge of her mouth denoted she wasn't pissed at him in the least. "*Our* bed?"

"Yes, *our* bed, sweetheart." He kissed the fight right out of her, then kept going. "You're practically moved in right now. All we need to do is get the rest of your things, and move your shit into my closet and dresser."

"But what about—"

He kissed her silent. "We'll talk about Jason and your mom soon. Until then, we're focusing on your healing. They know this already."

Crossing her arms over her chest, thinking over what Brycen had said, she turned to look at me and smirked. "I suppose we can do that. And, Rex." She took the two steps needed to bend over me, kissing my cheek before leaning closer to my ear. "Don't think you got out of telling me what the hell is going on with you and my friend. You might be a grizzly of a man, but I'm the mama protecting her kin." On a wink, she turned, and without giving Brycen another glance, she headed for the door.

"Later, Jana," I called, grinning. She threw a hand with a loose wave over her shoulder, and I shook my head as I peered at Brycen. "Happy for you, man." I offered him my fist, which he bumped with his.

"Thanks, man." He shrugged, smirking. "Don't think she'll let you off the hook, buddy. See you later."

"Later," I called to his retreating back.

I doubted she would let things go when it concerned her friend, but Jana also didn't have the slightest clue about all the shit I held close to the vest. If anyone other than Dalton and Brycen knew—because they were my bosses—no one had ever said anything. And when it came to women, relationships, and family, it was better that I kept those at arm's length. I'd given my whole self to one other person before—and it had cost me dearly—I wasn't going to make that same mistake twice.

thirty-three

Jana

WAKING up like this should be illegal. I mean really, what could be better than to be woken up by the warm body of a Grecian godlike man, calloused hands that knew just how to touch, a scruff that added just a touch of sexy roughness as he licked you until you came out of your mind, only for him to surround you before he possessed you mind, body, and soul?

"I love it when you do that thing that you do, with that other thing I like." I grinned as Brycen took my mouth, making me moan at the taste of me mixed with his sultry flavor.

Smirking down as he settled between my legs, giving me some of his weight, he said, "Oh yeah?"

Nodding, I added, "Yeah, but as much as I love you waking me with your mouth on my pussy, I'd much rather have—"

"This?" The bugger cut me off by thrusting himself in, deep and hard, making me arch into him. I couldn't hold back the moan as he rotated his hips, grinding his pelvis against mine. "Is this what you'd rather have?"

Generating a hiss from him as I clenched my muscles to

tighten my pussy's grip on his length, I bit my lip, then said, "Yeah, and I'm glad I'm the only one who gets you like this."

Upon my moving in two weeks ago, Brycen and I have been inseparable, but we'd also had a talk about deeper things—things we wanted for ourselves, for us...out of life. I suppose that's what happened when you stared death in the face. And that face had been Carson Platt. Needless to say, we'd vetoed the condoms.

"Fuck, baby, do that again," Brycen growled into the side of my neck, and I tightened that special set of muscles around him again. "Ungh. Christ, you're heaven."

Next thing I knew, he'd rolled us over so he lay on his back with me straddling him, never disconnecting our intimate bond.

It wasn't until I'd sat up and put my hands on Brycen's chest for leverage that I noticed it—white, large, shiny—beautiful. And on a very special finger I might add.

Sexy time forgotten for the moment; my heart stuttered as I struggled to stave off the tears that burned behind my eyes.

"Brycen," I whispered, my eyes meeting his gaze once I'd managed to pull them away from the sparkle that adorned my hand.

"You said you'd say yes whenever I asked," he whispered back as he did an ab curl to sit upright, cupping my face before pressing his lips against mine in a tender manner. "And I don't want to wait any longer to show the world I'm hopelessly, irrevocably in love with you. Marry me because you love me. Marry me because I can't live without you. Marry me because I'll live my life making your dreams come true like you're making mine, every damn day." I hiccupped through my tears as he smiled, his eyes filled with tears of his own and so much sincerity. "Marry me because life without you isn't even existing. I've lived it for nearly five goddamn days and four nights, and it damn well nearly killed me. We don't know how long we have in this lifetime, and I'm done waiting when there's something I can do—that *we* can do together—to make life as beautiful as it ought to be. Be my wife."

Cupping his cheeks with my hands, here he was, bare in more ways than us being skin-to-skin. He'd opened his heart to me like so many other times since we'd met and repaired all of the fractures in mine.

Brycen grinned wide, and although delayed in speaking my intent, my head was nodding as I told him my answer. "I would be honored, Brycen Matthews."

On a loud hoot, he crashed his lips to mine for an all-too-brief kiss. "I love you, Janice Elway, soon-to-be, Matthews." His eyes darkened with telltale lust the moment I clenched on his cock.

"I love you too, so get ready, I'm about to love on you a whole hell of a lot more, Mr. Matthews." I bit at his scruffy chin as he laughed, which then necessitated my dipping my tongue in one of those delectable dimples of his.

BRYCEN

She'd said yes.

Then she'd said *I do*.

And four months to the day since we'd met, the motherfucking world exploded around me—bringing things into a rose-colored perspective.

Surrounded by those we loved most—family and friends alike—during a backyard barbecue, I held my entire world in my arms, feeling blessed beyond belief.

"P-pregnant?" Eloise and Mom said at once as I stared down at my wife of two months, absolutely flummoxed.

Jana's eyes were solely on mine as she nodded her answer at the same question our moms had asked aloud, which shone in my eyes.

"Real—" I cleared my throat, swallowing the lump of elation mixed with subtle panic down and tried again. "Really?"

"Mm-hmm." She smiled wide, reaching behind her to grab my hand, then brought it down so my palm covered her belly, both her hands covering it as her eyes shimmered. "You ready for this, Daddy?"

Was I ready?

Hell to the yes, I was ready.

Terrified, yes.

Elated, sure.

Excited, beyond a doubt.

It was only natural when I pulled back after kissing the fuck out of my wife, Reina Boudreaux, MD had to open her mouth and say, "And that, ladies and gentlemen, is how they got where they're at."

Hoots and hollers followed, and there, in the middle of our backyard, surrounded by love and laughter, is when I knew I'd finally found the peace that had so long eluded me.

If you enjoyed *Night Hack*, please take a moment to let other readers know what you thought of Brycen and Jana's journey by leaving a review at your favorite retailer, or visit Goodreads. Thank you!

* * *

about the author

Born and raised in small-town Northern Ontario, Canada, Carey Decevito is a writer of erotic romance, paranormal romance, romantic suspense, and a member of the Ottawa Romance Writers. This lover of food will throw in a bit of heat, a dash of sass, a pinch of comedy, and a dollop of real-life experience to provide her readers with a story that will mess with their emotions from start to finish.

Family and friends are her lifeblood, but Carey also enjoys conquering the outdoors, sports, traveling, and playing tourist in Canada's National Capital region. When life gets crazy, she seeks respite through her writing and submersing herself in the latest addition to her library. If all else fails, she knows there's never a dull moment with her two daughters, her goofy husband, and their cat and dog who she swears are out to get her.

She is the author of *The Broken Men Chronicles*, *Essence Extracted Trilogy* and the latest *Nightshade* series.

facebook.com/carey.writes

instagram.com/carey_decevito

x.com/ItalRT4u

goodreads.com/ItalRT4u

bookbub.com/profile/carey-decevito

amazon.com/-/e/B0092HWSDY

also by carey decevito

Nightshade Series

Night Break

Night Shift

Night Hunt

Night Hack

The Broken Men Chronicles Series

Once Written, Twice Shy

Almost Forgotten

Play Me to Infinity

To Forgive & Hold Safe

A Heart's War

Essence Extracted Trilogy

Essence Derived

Essence Redeemed

Essence Surfaced

Collections & Anthologies

Love at First Sight: a first-in-series collection

www.ingramcontent.com/pod-product-compliance
Lightning Source LLC
Chambersburg PA
CBHW060359310726
48976CB00003B/883